ACROSS THE STONE BRIDGE

across the stone bridge

Tom O'Rourke

Quintus
An Imprint of ROMAN Books

Copyright © 2019 Tom O'Rourke

ISBN 978-93-83868-52-0

This is a work of fiction. Names, characters, places and
incidents are used fictitiously. Any resemblance to actual
events, locales or persons living or dead is entirely coincidental.

Typeset in Adobe Garamond Pro

First published in 2019

1 3 5 7 9 8 6 4 2

British Library Cataloguing in Publication Data
A catalogue record for this book is available from the British Library.

Publisher: Suman Chakraborty

Quintus
An Imprint of ROMAN Books
London | Kolkata
www.quintus-books.co.uk | www.quintus-books.co.in

Printed and bound in India by Replika Press Pvt. Ltd

Printed and bound in UK, USA and Australia by LSI

To Brenda;
an extraordinary woman,
and a wonderful mother to us all

contents

wonder

In the year 597 Pope Gregory of Rome sent his emissary Augustine to Ethelred, king of the Jutes in Britain; the two men met on the Isle of Thanet, in the place now known as Kent.

> *Eall is earfoðlic,*
> *eorþan rice,*
> *onwendeð wyrda gesceaft*
> *weoruld under heofonum*

The Aenglish *scop* taught him that song.

Strange sound, strange words, the meaning given to him in the Roman language:

> *All is troublesome*
> *in this earthly kingdom,*
> *the turn of events changes*
> *the world under the heavens.*

Disquiet.

Mid day gloom in the new growing season; light rain saturating old roots. The moist tang of salt and wet earth in his nose and mouth.

A cheerless dark breeze-blown day.

A furlong gaze; a boat is beached on muddy sand, sail furled, oars stowed upright against timbered sides. Curled black prows rebuff the grey air. Earlier the boat, royal-laden, rounded the headland of this isle of Thanatos, oars plunging through muddied Wantsum water to a slow relentless double drum beat.

More boats are grounded a long furrow from the royal boats. The boats have brought men women and children to be released into the early morning to bear witness. These people are Aenglish, Britons and others too, traders in this trading land, drawn from the Orient, from the lands under African skies, from the northern seas and from the southern seas, all drawn to this place by human curiosity, by a rumour heard in a drinking hall or in a market-place or at a hearth of women-talk; a man sent by a great chief of the Romans is come to speak with the king of this place.

Ethelbert, Jutish King, his Frankish queen Bertha. They sit in makeshift jewel-laden thrones placed upon a wooden platform set on the first level ground encountered beyond landfall. Red-robed king, gold-encrusted, gold shoulder guards, gold wrist-cuffs, heavy red garnet gold belt buckle inlaid with patterned filigree, wrapped around a still-lean waist. Bertha empurpled in a magenta cloak, queen-cloth, silk road, pinned by gold brooches at her thin shoulders. Suspended from her frail neck is a triangular pendant, a dark blue stone at its centre, gold-set, the stone hanging heavy from a chain of spun gold beads, each bead interwoven with oval and triangular multi-coloured stones set into each link.

"I see them, look there!"

A man, any man, everyman, shouts. Grey-black rocks sustain him. Many eyes follow his pointing arm.

Aneiran, Celt, young *scop*, poet of the tribe, sole survivor of the massacre at Catreath, allows his gaze to move from boats to king and queen and then, at the first shout, to the outstretched arm of the pointing man. He turns his lean profile westwards. A line of monks, two by two, perhaps in twenty rows, comes towards those who wait. Black-cloaked, hooded. The sound of distant human chants, low, the tone deep in the chest, a ragged dull harmony: all is absorbed by those who wait. Their progress seems set at an awkward angle to the low grey clouds.

Aneiran is Taliesin-tutored - Taliesin, mighty *word-breather,* annalist of the tribe – and is stuffed with knowledge for one so young. Ancient Celtic and Roman texts are stored in his prodigious memory.

Yes, he was there at the massacre of Catreath. The place where three hundred British warriors met their final end.

This is the reason he is present this day at a southern Aenglish warlord's meeting. He knows the war methods of Edelfrith, victor at Catreath. In the kingdom north of the Humber, the Aenglish battle-lord grows stronger by the day. Aneiran has been summoned here by the

Jutish King Ethelbert to speak, to say what he knows of this other warlord, but that meeting will be for another day. Today he stands in the first row of ealdormen and thanes - battle-strong, sword-wielding, shield-breaking, warlike men - to witness the arrival of Augustine, sent by the Roman Pope. He is *scop*; he carries no weapon. He is here to observe, to understand, perhaps to capture the vanishing memory in verse. His thinking mind greets them:

Advance, advance, come closer to me, strange messengers from the Roman lands.

Though not his own, he has studied the sacred texts of this cult whilst with Cuthbert and his monkish clan on Iona; all know of it since the Roman times. The faith of a naive powerless walking man, all compassion and meekness, a faith which promises life and joy everlasting in the next world, not this. Strength and valour, battle, live or die; these are the ways of my people, these are the acts that confer glory and gold in this life. Let the walking man preach his faith to the weak, those who will not fight.

Relentless their stride towards the assembled crowd. They hoist the huge burnished silver cross. Several red and gold tapestries depicting the Christ-figure – on some the figure is quiet, subdued, on others now resplendent, striding forth – are lifted up by the younger, stronger men. Similar images are painted onto plain boards. How must they feel, these strangers as they advance towards the royal group, sent by Gregory of Rome to teach the word of what they deem the true faith, to all of the people who inhabit this northern outpost of the old Roman empire? These angels in the north as Gregory called them, if the tale told to him is true.

A market place in Rome. Young Aenglish men, shackled, are lined up to be sold into captivity. So blonde, they attract the attention of a man, Gregory, who will one day be Pope. Who are these young men? Why, Your Excellency, they are Angles, pagans from the land of Deira in Britain. Ah, that such bright-faced folk should still be in the grasp of the author of darkness! They must therefore be saved 'de ira' - from wrath. So tall, so strong-limbed, such long golden hair, why yes, they are indeed like angels and they should be joint-heirs with the angels of heaven and brought into the life of Christ! And who is their king? It is Aelle. Then indeed Alleluias should be heard in their land. They deserve to receive the word of the Lord!

So the one called Gregory too is a wordsmith, a *scop*, a riddle-maker. He is well-matched with these Aenglish people.

Edelfrith it is who has overthrown Aelle; Bernician war-lord, blood-soaked victor of Catreath, cruel king of the Northern Kingdom,

Edwin's harasser. Three hundred men went to Catreath at dawn, fought ten times ten thousand, or so it seemed to me. Cynon, Cadfel, Blaen, Cynri and Cynrhain, Madog, Ieuan, Aeddan, Gwyn, Carardog, aye, all the rest of them too, their red-collared swords flashing in the clamorous morning sun, so many fated fallen heroes, all gone now under the hill.

The Celt studies the bowed tonsured head, bowed back, of the leader of this strange cult, this seemingly meek messenger from the land of the sun. He too has studied the ancient texts of this creed; he is young; his wild unrestrained poet's mind is sifting words:

As this man walks, does he see or sense the golden-haired seraphim - dense in full-bodied muscular maturity, each with mighty white swan-like wings, their eyes indifferent, distant, an alien beauty not of this world made - bursting forth in golden radiance flowing here there everywhere with torrential speed their flaming swords in arcs multi-coloured sweeping between all of these heathen hordes, sent to him here by his god to protect him?

Or as this man walks, does he see death before him?

Yes, Aneiran can now see fear in the eyes of these walking men. Perhaps their angels have deserted them? For all they know, they could be dead within moments, their first encounter with these new angels a fatal matter.

People begin to walk, stride, run towards the advancing monks. Two ragged lines rough-forming; many men, women and children on each side before the procession, all the way up to the royal platform, so that a human pathway is created.

Ealdormen and thanes of the king stand still on either side in formal rank before the royal couple. Sharp swords stay sheathed. A falconer stands amongst their ranks; hawk all tense pulsing body wrist-perched.

Other white birds cry out, soar, reel about crazily. They will feed where so many people have congregated.

Augustine has endured many long days inscribing sacred texts; he is tense, unsure. No obvious warrior, he. His eyes betray him. He raises his right hand; the monks stop suddenly. He turns askew - two or three short sharp precise instructions are barked out, his hands making urgent cutting strokes; the physical strain is clear to the fighting men who examine his every move.

The monk turns back to the human pathway set out before him; all are watching him, not a sound from the waiting crowd. He hesitates; then with determined stride he steps out on the final forty or so paces towards Ethelbert, King of the Jutes in the east of Britain. Behind him the monks begin another low chant, not quite hymn or song. A quiet *Alleluia! Alleluia!* faint at first, but grows stronger, more sure, already somehow inexorable, *Alleluia! Alleluia!* lifts up and outwards from their black-robed ranks and is heard by all of the mixed people gathered in this place. Slowly these relentless invaders - chanting hooded black-robed men - carrying a silver cross, bearing tapestries with figures woven in red and gold *quiet, subdued, resplendent!* chanting their strangely insistent relentless *Alleluia! Alleluia!* - walk through the final forty paces towards the king of the Jutes and the mingled tribes in this northern outpost of what was once the great empire of the Romans.

The white birds reel and cry, reel and cry above all the people assembled there. A vague sense of hidden claustrophobic frenzy fills the air.

All eyes are now on the leader as he reaches the platform. The chanting stops. He pauses not five paces from where Aneiran stands in the first rank, those nearest to the king. Aneiran thinks: what would mighty Cynon, bold hero of Catreath, ring-giver, shield-breaker, man-slayer, make of this man?

The king says nothing. He glances at Aneiran, who lifts his head slightly and looks towards the eyes of the holy man sent by Gregory, then back to the king. The king, too, looks closely at the downcast eyes of this emissary from Rome, here to preach the strange language of the peace-loving god, the faith of Ethelbert's queen, Bertha. He knows that this man, Augustine, has been besieged by doubts, has already returned once to Rome to beg not to be asked to continue with this improbable mission. Because the king knows, he respects the courage of this man who now stands in front of him. He will listen to any man who walks the land if he is sure his own status and the security of his people is not threatened. And this Augustine has spent many months at the powerful Frankish court from which he, Ethelbert, took his second wife who sits here beside him. The emissary is to be tolerated at all costs.

Bertha is wide-eyed, watchful; her work of many winters is now to be tested. Letters between her and Gregory and others too; her future and the future of her children by the Jutish king depend on what will unfold in the next moments. To her left stands Liudhard, Frankish bishop, protector of her faith in this land. He frowns through half-closed eyes. He has not relaxed for one moment since he stepped ashore into this barbaric land. There is a hint of blue in the roughly-shaved sagging skin of the bishop's jaw.

Ethelbert has ruled for many years, fought many battles, won more than he has lost. He fears magic. He has stipulated this first meeting shall be out of doors, so as to weaken any curse these black-cloaked hooded men might seek to place upon him.

The emissary speaks first, in strained Roman speech; a man next to him translates into the Frankish language. Augustine's voice is quiet, one tone, deferential though carries the natural rhythm of the words; there is real and immediate danger all around him.

"Great king of the Jutes, Ethelbert, we thank you for the courtesy so far shown to us poor monks sent by blessed Gregory to bring you the most glad news, which certainty will assure all who would receive it of eternal joy in heaven."

Ethelbert stares hard at Augustine; strange man uttering strange words.

"Let us offer up our prayer to God Almighty, creator of Heaven and this world, and to his Son who is Christ, saviour of all who will receive Him in this world, asking for eternal salvation of all those here present, both our own poor group of travellers and those who are here to receive us, who are those for whom we have travelled such a great journey and for whose sake we have come."

The monkish choir takes up the litany. An oddly beautiful sound swells out from their ranks, as the words of Augustine are repeated in eerie song.

The king understands this much: there is no immediate threat from these visitors. He nods to his ealdormen and thanes, smiles; ealdormen and thanes, like mannequins, nod, smile back. He turns, still smiling, to Bertha, a gentle question playing in his face. The Frankish queen already knows that this first encounter has gone well. Ethelbert is intrigued, curious. His men will not draw their swords. He has not turned away in disgust after the first exchange as he has on other first meetings with emissaries. Much rests on this meeting if the king's standing within the Frankish court is to grow. Rome, especially the one called Gregory, he who leads this special creed of the Christ-faith which has spread throughout its former empire, is a pathway to be cultivated.

The hymn finishes, the strange words fade out into the heavy damp air.

The king stands up.

"We thank you, men sent from Rome by Gregory; we will ponder over your strange words. Please be seated; speak to me and my people of this peaceful Christ of yours."

The talking starts.

Aneiran's mind wanders. He thinks of the previous evening, the feast in the king's hall - *so different from Mynyddog's Hall before Catreath!* - there he had witnessed many scenes; one image filters through his mind:

A juggler performs for the king. The juggler is a small well-made man, strong, nimble, light on his feet. Though young, his face is etched, rutted, his large features flexible, his short hair golden, curled. His wide mouth smiles broadly as his narrowed eyes fix on the blue red green clubs as he throws them into the air, behind his back, clubs, in a circle before him, clubs, in an arc above his head, clubs. Now he shouts *ah!* and *oh!* as if the clubs will tumble to the floor, but they do not. His giant moving shadow is cast onto the back timbers of the hall by the roaring hearth, as he moves effortlessly, to and fro, to and fro, clubs and shadows go tumbling through the warm air of the hall. Now his movements are faster, faster still; one by one he catches all of the clubs, red *oh!* green *oh!* blue *ah!* bows humbly and steps lightly away from the full-blazing hearth at the top of the hall and he goes back, goes back, goes back forever into the darkness of the hall, amidst much banging of mugs upon the heavy oak tables.

Still they talk.

Aneiran looks at the watchful men who surround the king and the emissary; their neutral faces immobile, swords, spears, half-axes held in belts or tied to their backs by cross-straps. Violent tools of the language these men understand, the language his people understand, the language the warriors of Catreath understood; in life mead, battle, gold and glory; in death – the soul must fend for itself.

He thinks of that other man, a walking man, physically a powerless man uttering simple words, unwar-like, who talked of the joy of life everlasting, but in the next world, not this. Why so? If one of these warriors hits me with his axe, this happens to me in this world, this moment. Should I raise my unprotected throat to his next blow? This is the world I feel, in which I feel, only this world.

He looks about him at the strange damp greyness of the day.

This field, this meeting; it is a strange place I find myself. How do the Romans say it?

Confluentia, conceptio....where the cross-currents meet.

He looks up through the low breaking clouds into the high vault of heaven. The released falcon now circles there; it has heard the call of the falconer, each circuit of its flight brings it tighter in on a new path, ordered and controlled. The centre holds as it spirals downward through its final descent. With sudden uplift of wide outstretched wings, the hawk slows, strikes - though gentle - onto the proffered wrist.

Whitegrey birds watch the predator and reel and cry...cry...reel and cry.

Pale disc of sun.

Pellucid light spreads over the dark earth.

He understands then: this is a poet's time, a poet's space.

The first cry goes out. Another. Many cries.

The roar of many people goes up around the field even as king and queen take a step back, as thanes and eoldermen reach for their swords, move towards the royal couple as if to protect them.

All – even king queen monk and bishop, their mouths agape in bewildered terror - stare in astonishment at a common man who stands a few rows back from the platform. A space has opened up between him and the people around him. He is enveloped, arrayed in redgold light and he is raised some six feet clear of the earth.

The poet watches with delight as this man, unsure, looks about at the people close to him, looks down bewildered at the displaced ground beneath his feet. See now, a woman on the other side of the platform, she too is enveloped, arrayed in red-gold light, she too is raised, and look, see that child and another, another, a multitude of men women and children from all the lands of the earth are lifted high above the field, all clothed in golden russet light, who, now, risen some sixty paces above the tiny wooden platform, wholly cut off from the awed and terrified earthbound crowd below them, look out over rainlit green fields rolling wolf-fur slopes teeming black cliffs sunglittering waters - their eyes, their features, their limbs as if full of a serene wonder

Torquino's Question

Beatrice di Folco Portinari died on the ninth day of June 1290.
On the eighth day of May 1300, an ambassador from Florence
journeys to the hill-top town of San Gimignano.

Before you and to your left sits the Podesta, the most important
man in this magnificent and rich hill-top Castle; behind him are arranged
the high-status civic dignitaries; the families already introduced to you as
the Braccieri and Ricardini, the Aldi and Baccinelli, Carpi, Useppi and
Marsili, all grown rich on agriculture, on saffron and Vernaccia wine, on
money-lending, all arranged in rank as you stand before them at the lectern.

You are momentarily dazzled by the early morning May sunlight
as it streams through the huge windows in front of you, above you, slightly
to your left.

Behind you on your right-hand side, lesser dignitaries are seated
on the benches. All in the room strain slightly forward, wait to hear the
words of the poet, now ambassador, rumoured soon to be one of the six
Priors of Florence, sent by Florence to address them.

The Hall is hushed.

You briefly note the freshly painted frescos of carousing and joust-
ing scenes which tell you plainly that for now this place is of the White
Guelph faction - your faction. This is the most important strategic strong-
hold in the region, it commands the heights of the Val D'Elsa. You are here
because it is important for political reasons that the people here should
think of themselves as *unem et idem* with Florence – one and the same.
You are to tell them that it is expedient for each of the cities of the Tuscan
League to hold a Parliament to elect a new Captain and then for all of the
appointed representatives of those cities to meet for the despatch of that
business. The historical record will show that your mission this day will
succeed.

You note the sensuous blue, red, green and gold of the robes of your audience; in passing, you note too a slight pulse under the right eye of the Podesta, de Tolomei of Siena, and wonder: what does this man think at this moment, this man who is rarely outranked in this place?

To the right of the Podesta, behind him, stands the guard previously introduced to you as Torquino. Tall, big-framed with square shoulders and a shaved bullet head, a raw, battle-scarred veteran at the age of twenty-four. You note how he shifts his weight restlessly from foot to foot, looks about him; it causes you to muse - *perhaps this soldier already prays this day of dry-as-dust procedural formality is over; perhaps he has a pre-arranged assignment for this evening with some feisty full-bodied woman who cares nothing for these politic formalities, perhaps a woman like Angelyka, black-eyed when naked and aroused, all tiny waist, flaring hips, soft yielding curves and lithe strong limbs, a woman whose senses and needs are fully alive, one who demands to take from this day whatever there is to be taken from it in the full glory of some life-affirming passion . . . .only then, satiated and all passion spent, will she allow him to tell her how he, Torquino, guard to the Podesta, witnessed in the flesh the day the ambassador from Florence came to talk to the people.*

You blink three times. In the space of five heartbeats you have triple sinned; to imagine that a woman might entertain such brazen lusty thoughts; to recall your mistress Angelyka again; to cast aside, in thought, your wife Gemma, mother of your children. You shall go to hell and eternal damnation if you do not find the path to your salvation. Your trained will grasps at, grips your wild imagination. You bring your mind back to the lectern in front of you. Slowly you remove the blue cloth cover of the red and gold-lettered vellum sheet.

Behind you in time: the Battle of Campaldino and the defeat of the Ghibellines, where you fought vigorously on horseback in the front rank of one hundred and twenty men, exposed to great danger; you were there too at the capitulation of the castle at Caprona. *La Vita Nuova*, those strange seemingly coded verses, has already made you known as a poet. Ahead of you in time, could you but know it, is the *Commedia*. There will be many trials too: the fiasco of your unbending two month rule as a Florentine Prior, your subsequent failed embassy to Rome and Pope Boniface VIII, your exile from Florence on the final victory of the Ghibellines under the auspices of the Angevin Charles. Then the fateful death sentence in absentia; your endless bitter wanderings, the hospitality offered to you in Verona and the Lunigiana and finally on to the city of mosaics and its symphony of colours. The last abortive journey to Venice and your fatally stricken flight back to Ravenna, like one who has voyaged out upon lost seas, never to return.

This future life is unknown to you. Now at this moment you look up at your unmoving, silent waiting audience. You half-raise your left arm and reach for the cup of water, half-noting the red and yellow glaze of the ceramic cup. You glance once more at the vellum sheet in front of you, idly record the date at the foot of the formal document. And another unbidden thought strikes you then, as if an unseen silver silent arrow has pierced deep into your heart. On this day next month, she who has devoured your stricken heart, she whom your mind beholds in glory, shall have been gone from the sorrows and sad joys of this unredeemable world for ten full years.

You physically shudder at this imagined blow; for an instant you close your eyes as a riot of despair rolls through you; for an instant terror is in your face, almost unseen.

One man alone in the Hall sees it: Torquino, the soldier, the fighting man, who for the rest of his long life will tell nobody of the stark terror he sees in your face at this moment, even though he will never forget it. Sometimes, now and then, in his last years after many battles, perhaps momentarily alone in the back room of a tavern at night, his belly full of Vernaccia wine and his booted feet up on the stove, his leather waistcoat, unbuttoned, hanging loosely around his thickened girth, the old mercenary will stare into the embers of the fire and remember again this moment and wonder: what was it that caused such fear to come into the face of the Florentine ambassador, that man who became the great poet? And then he will slowly stand up, lean over to rake up the embers in the stove, tenderly straighten his battle-weary spine even as he draws a hand down his scarred embattled face, will step heavily across the stone-flagged floor and go through, go through to the main room of the Tavern, the embers of the fire slowly fading as the muslin cloth curtain falls back into place behind him.

You steady yourself against the lectern and recover yourself instantly. The hawk-like profile turns towards the Podesta, towards history, towards-------?

"Good people of San Gimignano . . ."

gateway

The city waits.

The news is that the rebels will march on the Walls today, perhaps tomorrow, certainly before the end of the week. The boy-king Richard himself has moved into the Tower until the crisis is over.

The customs man looks out of the east window of his chamber above Aldgate beyond the spire of St Buttolphes, across the haphazard dwellings, patched fields and higgledy garden plots towards Mile End and the rebel encampment. This is one of the few routes into the walled city if and when they decide to come in. Both of the portcullis gates have already been lowered; most people are indoors.

He looks at the three heavy iron bolts on the chamber door. He will lie low, keep out of the room till after dark; this place above the Gate is too exposed. So he will move about this evening quietly, give nobody cause to question him. He may have won some praise as a court verseman, but he is also a royal tax collector, and already there have been reports of on-the-spot executions – beheadings, terrible slaughters – of tax men in Rochester and Deptford. The people are on the march, and nobody can know how matters might work through.

His head is aching, his back is sore – what was it Talbote the merchant had said to him?

"If you spent a tenth of the time turning that sharp eye of yours to your own affairs as you do to mine, the king's purse would be much the better for it!"

They are all grown bold in these febrile times; the wool customs office down in the Port of London hosts a daily slanging bout, merchant after merchant disputing this return, that return.

But he is a resilient man – and to lie low does not mean to hide. He will drink ale.

He chooses the coarse heavy robe. Brown and hooded, even though it is just gone mid-summer eve; picks up the soft black hat from a chair, turns the heavy key in the lock and descends through the tower's spiral stone staircase down to street level.

He turns right, stays within the City Walls.

It is quiet on the streets; he will keep away from those places in which he is known as a taxman and take a cart towards Eastcheap and the Bridge and go down to the Vintry – get back amongst the merchant wharfs he knows from his own childhood. He will seek the company and the conversation of his father's people - the wine traders, for amongst them he will not be betrayed. Two piggins of ale, then home.

He climbs up into the first patched-up cart that stops for him, the old nag turns her head lazily and watches him as he clambers up onto the rough-hewn bench.

"The Crane in the Vintry, by way of Wall brooke . . ."

The driver nods in response and they set off at walking pace through the streets of Aldgate, down St Katherine Colman and onto Lombard Street.

The rhythmic clack of iron hooves mingles with the sound of iron shutters clanging shut; the city turns inwards, prepares to weather the coming storm. It smells of stale beer and roasting meat, dung and piss. The evening mid-summer sun still casts a high light, catches the edge of the rusting shop-signs, leaves a curious scarlet-orange skillet of colour on the various sloped and slanted brick walls of the squashed-in shops, exposes the peeled lime of their door-fronts.

Slowly the rocking cart rattles past St Mary Woolnoth on his left; as it does so the old Norman bell strikes for Vespers; the vital sounds seem to spread out and fill the space in Lombard Street. A few more tired paces and the nag turns left into Wall brooke, begins the steady downhill trot towards the river-bank.

Soon enough the taxman sits at a bench in the main room of the Crane with a half-full piggin of ale in front of him. The ride on the cart had been pleasant, if too warm, dressed as he is in the heavy brown robe. The mid evening sun continues to cut in straight slices through the long high windows; green-blue leaded panes; blue-silver dust-motes swirl about lazily in the space around him. The rugs are faded, threadbare in places.

There are fewer people here than he had expected. The angry rebels have cast their long shadow over the city.

Before him are three men, drunk, who shout at each other in slurred voices. At the table opposite him a young man and woman speak intimately, though in urgent, secret tones. Across the room he can see a party of women, all ages, tidily but not richly dressed, some speak loudly, some laugh, others watch, several already red-faced with wine.

In another corner a gang of young men plot something, glance furtive looks across the room to the party of women.

Behind the bar the host, a big bald man with a damp white towel thrown over his shoulder, his sleeves rolled up over his elbows, watches the room.

Now the man speaks to the woman at the bench opposite, stands up, shouts:

"One of these days, you will stop giving me commands and listen to me!"

He lifts his eyes and his arms up to heaven and stamps out.

The man in the brown robe watches the deserted woman as she turns back to the table, stares at it for a moment, moves her leather cup of wine in small circles in front of her. Then she raises her eye-brows and shakes her head, stands up and walks across to the long benches where the women's party is in full flow. Loud bawdy laughter now spills out around the room; one of the older women shouts across at the young lads:

"Why not come and join us boys?"

The youths say nothing; then one of them mutters something, so only those on his table can hear, and then they all start to laugh, to snigger. But they are shy, gauche, unsure of themselves.

Now the woman who had shouted to them turns back to the table, states loudly,

"Ha! Even if they could get it up, they wouldn't know where to put it anyway!"

The older women at the table all sway and rock with laughter, looking at each other, guffaw, some beat the table before them.

The speaker looks across to the man dressed in the brown robe.

"You at least look as if you might have a notion of how to treat a lady. Come and join us?"

He looks at her calmly, a little surprised by the direct invitation. Phillippa has been out in the country with Thomas at Gaunt's court for several weeks. He is alone in the city with its menacing troubles. He is pressed upon by his fears; perhaps it is this state that causes him to take risks he would not usually take.

"Very well then, I shall join you."

He picks up his hat and his ale and moves across to the table and benches where the women of all ages are sitting.

"Good evening Ladies!"

He lifts his wide black hat, bows, sweeps the hat across his knees in a graceful manner.

The women are all false agog with coos and cries, batting their eyes at him.

"Hooo, a right gentleman you've found here, Aly! Right elegant looking man too!"

"He's handsome. Look at that forked beard – he's a cunning one he is . . ."

A big buxom woman looks at her friend and says loudly

"Aye, he looks like he could go all night if I was allowed to sets him off in the right direction!"

The women laugh again, some slap the bench in front of them.

He throws his hat onto the bench, sits down, amused. He feels no sense of shyness, of reserve. He is comfortable in the company of women, especially now when they have finished their working day and simply want to laugh with each other in the dusty evening light, talking their world into existence.

"So ladies, may I ask why you are here this evening? Do you not fear the rebels?"

The woman who has first called to him now speaks up.

"Why, its Meg's birth feast today, and we've all come to witness it with her. As for the rebels – look at us, not one of us is worth more than a pound of pennies! Yet we are sterling folk; what we say is what we mean, not like the fine people; what they say is rarely what they mean! So the rebels, they're our people, and if they come in we might well join 'em!"

She smiles at her friends around the table.

"Now you've turned up at just the right time. Feel free to ask us, sir, any question you have always wanted to ask a clutch of beauties like us – anything you want!"

He sits across from the woman who speaks. She is no longer young, her face is deeply lined around her green eyes which have laughed long and often. Her black hair has grey in it; from her ears dangle bright fools-gold ear-rings; her figure is full, life-affirming. Her clothes are simple yet elegant; he guesses that she is a waiting-on-lady for the wife of a rich wine merchant in one of the big houses here. Maybe this is true of all in her party. Perhaps they serve the Bordeaux wine merchants here in the Vintry?

She looks at him assessing her, winks at him, then speaks up to the rest of the table.

"Mind you, anything too personal I may have to tackle quietly with you in the back room!"

They all laugh again.

He stands up.

"What should I call you, madam?"

"You may call me Alyson."

"Well Alyson, good ladies, there is a question I have always wanted to ask my wife, but have never so far had the courage . . ."

"Uh-oh, no good coming to us for a view, not one of us have rolled with you . . . yet!"

Again, they all laugh.

He smiles, speaks in his best orator's voice.

"The question is just this: what is it that women most desire in this life?"

Now all the women are quiet for a moment, and look at each other. Then they all begin to speak at once.

Alyson says

"A moment, a moment first! Courtesy demands that the good gentleman buys a jug of wine for the table before we reveal to him the answer to his question!"

He gestures to the host - a jug of wine for the table, and a large piggin of ale for him.

The women, talking amongst themselves, banish him to the back room. He is there still thinking about mobs, doors and iron bolts when they call him back into the main room of the Tavern.

Alyson stands at the table.

"We all agree that the first part of the answer to your question is that there are as many desires a woman wants in this world as there are women. So your question is the wrong question. It should be: what is it that each woman most desires in this life? Not all women – it's not one answer for all. But we have some answers for you . . . you go first Meg, it's your feast day."

Meg is young, she is enjoying her birthday with her friends.

"I like elegant clothing and fine jewellery and hope to find a fine handsome husband one day."

Some of the women nod, others look at each other, they're not so sure, dubious.

"And you Sal, what do you desire most in the world?"

"I like to see honourable actions between people."

Now all the younger girls want to throw their halfpenny into the pot.

24

"My greatest desire is happiness, to be happy and for others to be happy with me."

"A good lusty man in bed!"

"To be married many times!"

"To have many healthy surviving babies."

"To be flattered and pleased."

"For a man to be attentive to me, to fuss over me."

Now the oldest woman at the bench waves her hand, she wants to speak.

"All this you say is well and good and I said just the same when I was young as you are. Now there is only one thing I want in my life, more important than anything else: I want to be free to be as I am, without criticism of any kind from any man."

And several of the older women agree, they think this is right.

Now the man looks at Alyson.

"And you Alyson, what is your answer?"

Alyson looks at him, hesitates, then she says, "I claim some experience in the ways of this life, stranger. I have been married five times. Two of them were right good men, and often I treated them terrible, may God rest their souls and forgive me. And two of them were brutes, horrible small-minded monsters, and I wish to God I had had no dealings with those men. My fifth husband now is a young man, Jan King is his name; he has a ready wit and a ready temper too. He reads books, and is right lusty."

She pauses, suddenly shy.

"He is twenty, and I am forty. I hope to God that by means of my own natural wild ways I might accommodate him, and that we might go forward together for the rest of our lives."

She pauses again. Her voice has become quieter as she speaks. Now the joshing has all fallen away; her face is flushed.

"For I wisheth us selven two to haf joynte soveraynetee
Over us selven in this our lyfs and over our soules for al eternitie."

*

It is after dark. In such good company too many piggins have been taken before he left the women; his thoughts are mild, scattered. A few hard-packed torches burn down slowly in their beckets above the shop-signs. In the weak light, he sees a man hangs back in the dark near the portcullis gatehouse, one who, at the sound of the cart as it creaks and clacks back down Aldgate, steps out into the clear moonlight.

With some surprise, he sees it is not William Duerhirst, porter of the Gate and known to all in Aldgate, but another William, Tonge the alderman.

The two men stare at each other for a few moments. Tonge speaks first:

"Do not tell your royal friends at court what you see me do tonight, and I promise you in return I will not tell the waiting mob that a tax-man sleeps in the room above their heads."

Tonge holds a finger to his lips, the question still in his face.

The tax-man poet looks at the alderman; he is weighing both the odds and the trustworthiness of this man. Then he nods and walks over to the tower door, even as Tonge begins to turn the first of the heavy wheels which will lift the portcullis on each side of the Gate.

The poet reaches the door, glances across at St Buttolphes. Through the opening Gate he can see the unmoving shadows of a vast crowd of men silhouetted against the church wall, most with burning torches, some with flags, some with banners, in a line stretching down St Buttolphes Lane as far as his eye can see. He can hear no sound from them.

Deftly he inserts the heavy double-handed brass key into the old lock, opens and closes the door, locks it again, and without making a sound, races up to his chamber on the first floor of the Gatehouse. Once he is in the room, he slides the three heavy iron bolts into place and stands against the thick wooden door and away from the slightly open window facing east. His heart is pounding in his ears.

He can hear the sound of many voices approaching the Gate, see the glow of burning torches throw the flicker of light dancing up and down the far wall of his chamber. Iron objects strike and drag against the stone walls of the tower as they start to stream into the city. The voices are growing in volume, there is a frenzied madness about them as they pass through the arch under his chamber. He picks out phrases from the drunken guttural animal howls laced with curses and obscenities.

"Get the bastards! Head for the Tower, burn the palaces! Look for the Flemings, all the fucken foreigners, root 'em out, cut their fucken heads off! We march for Tyler and Jack Straw! No more poll tax, burn the poxy tax-men and all the fucken money-men, kill the boy-king himself – to the Tower! The Tower! The Tower!"

Drunken laughter rolls through much of what they say.

It is become a roar of drunk mad men swarming into the city towards God knows what.

He crushes his full weight back against the door, places his doubting trust in the iron bolts. He is sweating, his breathing comes hard...

voyager

"That fool Percy has been back in the stockade for the last two hours, he's gone to see De La Warre, doubtless explains to that tyrant the success or otherwise of his mission. I do not like the look of it; his troop is much reduced, the surviving men look haunted . . . and he had a prisoner with him on his return – an Indian woman, high status, distraught – something terrible has happened out there, and Percy was the least capable man to have been sent out on such a mission."

Rolfe paces up and down the primitive shack, his hair tied back, his shirt unbuttoned at the neck, sweat patches, sleeves rolled up to the elbows. He is smoking a blue clay pipe; a pungent, evil smell fills the thatch and daub structure.

"I tell you, William, those two together will be the death of this colony and of all those within it. The natives grow more dangerous with each passing day. It is not war but laws that are needed here. Discipline, law, order, no one allowed to take one step out of place. Gates was right, and may he soon return. Our future and the future of this enterprise, this new world, depend upon it . . ."

Strachey looks into the weary face of his friend. The acrid smoke curls about him. He coughs.

"Must you smoke that bloody weed?"

Rolfe looks at his friend, smiles.

"It's good for you! The physics say it clears out all bad humours from the body!"

Strachey shakes his head. Now he thinks of what Rolfe has said about those who govern this small world in the swamp.

"We have not come so far, survived so much, to lose sight of why we are here. All that you say is true, and God knows what has gone on out there in the last few days; maybe we will hear all about it soon enough."

Still Rolfe paces the floor.

Low embers burn in the central stone hearth in the shack. Outside of the hut it is late evening in early August, the humid heavy air is full of biting insects.

Strachey looks across at his friend.

"Those seeds you planted, the Indian tobacco – what do you really make of it?"

Rolfe spits into the mud floor.

"Too harsh by far, even for my taste."

He pauses.

"There is a fine, mellow, tobacco I tasted once – part of the prize coming out of a captured Spaniard sailing up out of the Spanish Islands. It's grown there; they guard it on pain of death. One day I will get my hands on that seed and I will plant it here. It will take root; I will make my fortune."

Strachey laughs.

"Tobacco plantations in this swamp! Will you never tire of these dreams of yours? And the Indians, what about them? Perhaps one day you will make them your family, and you will all live in a merry harmony?"

He stops speaking, his mind has wandered.

"But why not dream? We are lucky still to be alive, you and me."

Rolfe knows his friend thinks of the *Sea Venture*, the terror of the storm, the Bermudes times.

"What progress on your letter?"

Strachy reaches into the battered leather pouch placed on the table.

"I've completed it, tried to record some of it . . . that tempest, by Christ, may God be thanked for our deliverance from it!"

He offers the parchment to Rolfe, who stops pacing up and down, reaches for it, snatches it from Strachey's hand and flings himself onto the battered divan set snug against the mud wall.

He reads for a few moments. Plumes of rancid blue smoke fill the space he sits in.

"William, this is remarkable. I truly feel as if I am back in that dreadful hole. I am astonished even now that we all survived it!"

He reads more, raises an eyebrow, looks up at his friend, quotes:

'*...a dreadful storm and hideous began to blow from out the north-east, which swelling and roaring it were by fits, some hours with more violence than others, at length did beat all light from Heaven...*'

" . . . this really does begin to return me to . . ."

There is a loud rap on the door of the cabin. A voice outside.

"Mr Rolfe! Captain Percy requests your attendance immediately."

Strachey strides across, throws open the door. A trooper stands

29

there in a faded old red and gold tunic. The old queen now gone.

"Good evening, Mr Strachey, Sir. Good, that saves me a job. You are also requested to attend Captain Percy, there have been events you both need to know about."

Strachey looks across at Rolfe, shrugs his shoulders. Rolfe, exasperated, gets up, throws the parchment onto the table.

Together they walk across to the main cabin, the only timber structure within the stockade fences. The evening is still humid, heavy; the stinging flies swarm around the lit torches. Beyond the fences of the three cornered fort, the thick swampy foliage threatens to encroach upon, to engulf the encampment. They exchange glances; both have noted many extra guards have been posted against the main gate and along the perimeter fencing.

Rolfe walks up to one of the guards.

"What is it, why so many men?"

The young man is a survivor of the last few months; he is now older than his years; he looks at Rolfe for a few moments with a cool, sullen regard. Rolfe stares back; he has noticed this mannerism in the younger men, this second thinking about how to address a person who speaks to them. All of the rules that applied in the old world barely apply here, in this place. Barely. The young fellow looks away, thinks better of his first thought, does not look at Rolfe as he speaks.

"There's been trouble."

He says no more. Rolfe, now with Strachey standing beside him, pulls back the main gate slightly, looks out into the heavy air, thick with stinging insects. A smell of wet alien foliage rests very close, the vital stink of swamp. An incessant insect whispp crkk whispp crkk whispp crkk fills the hanging air. One tone, high-pitched.

"This hellish noise, does it ever . . . ?"

Rolfe stops speaking, his complaint unfinished.

He thinks he has heard something, an anguished scream, checked in mid cry.

"Did you hear that?"

He looks out over into the deepest part of the jungle.

Strachey lifts his head, looks around him.

"I can hear only these damn insects . . ."

"No, not that. Something else, something . . . a human, in pain."

"I heard nothing."

Rolfe stares out into the uninviting night; the heaviness seems to thicken by the moment.

"Perhaps it was nothing, some strange night bird. Let's get over to Percy . . ."

Captain Percy stands at the centre of the timbered room, propped up against a chair, still in his sweat-drenched tunic, all but done in. Rolfe sees that he is alone.

"Where is his Lordship?"

"Feverish and ill-humoured again, taken back to the ship to recover."

"And your mission?"

"A success, by any estimate. I destroyed the village, burnt the crops, killed all those who did not manage to escape. When I got back, I rowed out to see him on the ship. His Lordship is pleased. He will have his revenge for poor Ratcliffe, for the starving time they forced upon us here."

He looks over to the two men.

"But of course you were not here then, cannot know the horror of it . . ."

His voice trails away.

Strachey, like Rolfe, is thinking of other horrors, of certain death in the midst of a tempest on the open ocean, all undertaken in the hope of reaching this strange new world, this colony in Virginia.

Percy looks directly at Strachey and Rolfe; his cheeks are sunken, his eyes dark-ringed; the mission has taken a heavy toll upon his spirit.

Neither asks him to recall the horror of what happened to Ratcliffe, nor his memory of the siege of James Fort. They had both seen enough of the abominations of starvation when they had finally arrived with the remnants of Gates's party, nine months late, after the wreck of the *Sea Venture*.

"I called you here for a reason. There has been cruelty, and I think it is not finished yet. I am all done in . . . I hope that you can do something to stop it."

They may think him a fool, but for an Oxford man and a papist, both know him to be a good man, though weak, swept about by the currents of life and by those stronger than him. Both men can see too that he is close to collapse.

Rolfe says, "Speak up George, what is it?"

"I left Paspahastown in flames, as I told you. I took with me one of their queens, a wife of one of their chiefs - maybe the cunning old fox himself - and her two children . . ."

Rolfe and Strachey glance at each other.

"By the time I got all to the boats, the men were murmuring, discontent, not happy with the Indian prisoners . . . "

He trails off, lost in some thought.

A sense of dread suddenly hangs in the air.

Strachey urges, "What happened?"

"They would not listen to me, threw the children overboard, shot them there in the water . . ."

His head drops, his long thin hands and fingers come up to his lank hair.

"By Christ, but life in this new world is a brutal business!"

Rolfe pales, suddenly remembering . . .

"And the wife of the chief, George, where is she?"

"It was all I could do to return here with her alive. The men wanted to kill her too. But His Lordship was not pleased that I brought her back. He asked me to leave, wanted to discuss something with Davis without me there . . ."

He looks hard at Strachey and Rolfe.

"Enough brutality for one day. Rouse the Council. See if something can be done to stop it; if nothing else she will be a good ransom in the months to come."

There is a sudden loud pounding on the wooden door.

All three men start up.

George Percy stares at the door, momentarily wide-eyed, as if Fate itself stands there, impassive, pounding against it. He looks wearily at Strachey and Rolfe.

"Open it, let us see what final delight crowns the day . . ."

The door is thrown open. Captain John Davis, stately, plump, with dishevelled hair, muddied red and yellow tunic, king's man, commands the space. Percy knows this fellow. During the starving time he and thirty men stayed away, survived with full rations outside of the fort.

The set face of Davis betrays an unsettled satisfaction; the bloodied scabbard hangs loosely by his side.

"No need to worry, George, old fellow, your unfinished business is now . . . finished."

Smiling, he strides confidently into the cabin.

*

Once again, he brings the glassed candle closer to the title at the head of the page:

A True Reportory of the Wreck and Redemption of Sir Thomas Gates, Knight, upon and from the Islands of the Bermudas: His Coming to Virginia and the Estate of that Colony Then and After, under the Government of the Lord La Warr, July 15, 1610, written by William Strachey, Esquire

That this parchment with its fine calligraphy and many stains should have travelled over the rough oceans to this spot here on this oak table in the middle of England. For a passing moment, he feels the full width and weight of that thought: deep low roar of absent lost seas, lowly roaring always.

He studies the words once more.

'Here, the glut of water (as if throttling the wind erewhile) was no sooner a little emptied and qualified, but instantly the winds (as having gotten their mouths now free and at liberty) spake more loud and grew more tumultuous and malignant.'

glut

A rich full word.

glut

He looks at the second manuscript at his left side. It is newly completed. He searches through the first pages of the ink-covered parchment. He scratches a few words there.

And gape at wid'st to glut him.

He scatters a fine-grained sand, waits a moment, shakes it gently from the page.

A tempest. Our tiny globe of a world, now made more so by the Pisan and his telescope; our little history repeated on this little island of a world, not once or twice but three times. At all levels of man's estate. As ever and forever, amen.

The staff is broken.

He brings the candle back to the *True Reportory* parchment, searches for words again:

'Nothing heard that could give comfort, nothing seen that might encourage hope.'

His work is done. Let them make of it what they will.

33

hero

He stands on the Quarter Deck with his two feet firmly planted, looking slightly to his left so as to correct the blindness in the right eye; his left arm is raised.

The dark-blue wool cloth of his rear-admiral undress uniform, with its bright epaulettes, its stand-up collar and button-back lapels, adorned down the left side with the four orders of chivalry - Knight of the Bath, Order of the Crescent, Order of Ferdinand & Merit and Order of St Joachim – would not deceive a potential one on one opponent. He appears to be a slight man, frail, sickly-looking. A scar, ill-stitched by the light of a puckering candle, runs haphazardly down the forehead to the impotent right eye; the right arm gone after the elbow, the hair prematurely white. A fine spray thrown up by the gentle sea-breeze repeatedly caresses his pale face.

He has to raise his voice, but even now his voice is calm, steadfast, as if he is in some other place.

"Bring her round, bring her round . . . be ready . . . be ready . . ."

The British Flagship moves as if in the middle of a roiling dense forest, oak-timbered, great towering sails lazily flapping all around form an off-white shifting canvass roof, many-layered, so dominating this space that the grey sky can be seen only in patches. He sees that they are right up between the timbers of the bow of the *Bucentaure,* the top deck of which rises and falls in front of him, and the stern of the *Redoubtable*, just yards away, already turns about, looks to ram them. The cannon of the French ships are momentarily useless, the British ship is through and betwixt them, it breaks the line.

Thousands of men, hearts racing, eyes wide open, teeth ground in set faces, wait for that left arm to drop.

And then it falls.

For a few moments, there is total silence. Then all senses are concussed by the sound of ten thousand thunders. The air dances crazily as the big guns of the British first-rater open up from its left flank, sending a full treble-loaded broadside down the full length of the *Bucentaure,* bow to stern, and the same from its right flank into the *Redoubtable,* stern to bow.

Like some unholy breath of an evil god, one and a quarter tons of lead balls with body-tearing chain and link-shot howl through the masts, rigging and canvass of the *Bucentaure.* Immediately engulfed in a swarming storm of small metal balls, nails, chainlinks, shards of glass, rocks and wooden splinters, men are instantly swept backwards and sideways like dust before a broom.

As the British Flagship begins to move away from the full perpendicular, from directly behind the French Flagship, an action which occupies a period of no more than ninety seconds, there is time for the left arm to fall again, for another full treble-shot load to rip again through the main decks of the *Bucentaure* and *Redoubtable,* just like the exhalation of some old bored god. Again, dust before a broom.

Ears still ringing, the smell of gunpowder, fresh splintered oak and salt-sea full in his nose, blue smoke thinning before him, the slight well-dressed man turns to his younger colleague, then looks to his right, gestures casually with his left arm as the taller man bends down to hear his words.

"Have a mind to the French second-rater. He will ram us, will come straight at us. Tell the men to expect to engage; fire into them even as they come into us, we'll de-mast her before they do us . . ."

The younger man nods and, close to the ear, speaks quietly, using the appropriate tone.

"Yes, my lord, I see his purpose. Well, we shall not wait for him."

Even as he speaks, he gestures to the still intact Wheel-house, indicates that the stern of the British Flagship should turn into the French second-rater.

As the ship comes about all on-board can see the French troops and sailors line the sides of the *Redoubtable*; it is clear that this will be a hand to hand fight, and already the British gunners in the two lower decks run up to the top deck, armed; they scream they shout, they prepare to engage the Frenchmen in the frenzied death-dance. There is a splintering collision as the two ships engage, even as the cannons on the top deck of the British Flagship fire into the rigging of the other ship, barely yards apart. Now the rigging is entangled, there are gaps in the many-layered canvass roof, grey clouds can be seen momentarily. It is clear that the French ship has the worst of it . . . but its men do not back off, the macabre death-dance begins.

The slight-built commander in the blue uniform ignores the screams, the brutal howls, the flash of steel as the rolling maelstrom careers about in front of him; men fall - he blinks as his secretary John Scott stumbles at his feet, then looks away - he brings the small telescope up to his left eye, scans the horizon, assesses the situation in seconds.

Leading the Leeward Squadron, *Royal Sovereign* is ahead of him, to the right and south of his position, having already broken through the line. He suspects that Collingwood may have crippled the Spanish Flagship *Santa Anna* with his first broadside through the stern and down the length; he has now swung around to attack the beam of the Spanish Flagship, even as three or four of the Spanish ships close in on him; the rest of the Leeward Squadron will be with Collingwood soon enough.

Good.

It is all going as he has planned. He has broken the line at several points. It will be a pell-mell battle, will involve more ship-to-ship engagements just like this one. In such a battle, he believes the greater seamanship and better morale of the British forces will prevail, inevitably.

He notes that the *Temaraire* closes in on the far side of the *Redoubtable;* with luck she will catch the French troops and sailors on the top deck with a broadside before they can engage with the crew of his ship.

He understands himself to be a man of strong will, drive and ambition. He places his trust in reason. He is sure he will win this battle. He believes his victory to be God's Will, that he and his name shall receive great glory when it does happen. His planning has been meticulous, completely based upon rational assessment and his intuitive understanding of the quality of his opponent, the man he faces, Villeneuve. He expects the British fleet to capture at least twenty French and Spanish ships during the engagement.

He also expects to die.

He has left a written request that Emma and Horatia be taken care of by a donation from the public purse. He wonders if they will do this, in all the circumstances.

Last evening, he has written a final prayer to God. He believes he has done his duty as England expected. His reputation, carefully cultivated by himself since he was first made captain at the age of twenty, is secure. His entirely rational policy of sending anonymous accounts of his actions in battle to the press, a policy decided upon by him after the authorities failed to duly take note of his influential involvement in early engagements, has paid off. The people all think him a hero.

He expects it all to be as his reason dictates.

At the crux of this murderous sea-battle that will decide world naval supremacy for at least the next one hundred years, he walks about the Quarter Deck as if strolling through the park at Merton; his mind is quite clear, quite rational; this is the way it should be, the way he wants it to be.

He is content.

A French sniper, an anonymous man of apparently no account who will also die this day, is somehow still perched high up in the blasted entangled rigging of the *Redoubtable*. He aims his musket down and across the Quarter Deck of the British Flagship *Victory*, sees the dark blue wool coat, the tails and breast lined with white silk twill, the left shoulder gaily bright with an as yet un-bloodied epaulette . . .

*

Three weeks or so later another man walks through the middle of a dense wood in the north of England.

Though it is mid afternoon in November, the trees, thickly-packed, slope down steeply away to his left into night-time dark; to his right, the hillside continues to rise, the trees become sparser. His path is carpeted by russet autumnal leaf-fall. He has passed no other soul for the last hour. This place feels like some well-kept secret, a magical land where trolls or spirits or heroes, or all of them together, might gather if a man is minded to consider such matters.

He too is lean, slightly-built. His hair is receding at the front though carefully combed forward; his eyes large, nose prominent, eyebrows full, mouth sensuous. Perhaps it is not quite the face of a poet, not quite as this tiered society expects the face of a poet to look.

He has walked up out from Grasmere through the silence of Grisedale Tarn, ignored Helvellyn by Dollywagon and walked through farmland down to Genridding and on to Aira Falls, taken the steep path behind the Falls to the good track through Ulcat Row and circled back through these woods; he intends to press on to the view over Ullswater under Gowbarrow, back down to Patterdale and then the post-carriage home.

He thinks of the long poem just finished; he has said much in it and it will not be published whilst he yet lives. He feels the main work of his life is ahead of him. He is thirty five years of age – half-way through his ordained three score years and ten – time enough for more good work to come, even great work. The latest edition of the *Ballads* with Coleridge is just now published – again in the *Preface* he has explained his thinking - he will rescue the language, bring it nearer to the language of men. His work so far has been met with hostility or indifference.

But these matters are not his main concern now as he walks on through the deep wood. His mind is agitated. Money worries assail him. Mary is expecting their third child. The loss of his brother. They say too that Buonaparte is camped in Brittany with an invasion force, waiting for the arrival of the joined forces of the French and Spanish fleets coming up out of Cadiz to carry him to victory across the Channel. The dictator plans to overwhelm Great Britain, to take these islands before turning towards the north and east.

He muses: *what then for Annette and his daughter Caroline alone over in Calais?* His young daughter was a delight when he had met her for the first time, two, no, three years ago, a time of tranquil suns and a gentle heaven over the sea.

He pauses for a moment, leans back against a raised bank of turf on his right side, deep in thought. His younger brother John, proud captain of the East Indiaman *Earl Of Abergavenny*, drowned off Weymouth Bay, going down with his ship just a few short months ago. He has been with John on this walk in the past. Without effort he can feel his brother's spirit close to him, now, in this place. His own spirit is subdued, oppressed by a sadness that will not leave him. He thinks of his time in France, the hopes of the Revolution, the devastating reality of the Terror.

He shakes his head, slightly irritated by the recall of his own experience. He stands up straight, strides on.

Ahead of him he can see a faint rose hint of sun, filtered through autumnal leaves; already the darkness down to his left is thinning out, growing paler.

Soon enough he is walking over higher ground, slightly breathless, striding out under Gowbarrow. Just then the length of the lake and its environs opens out before him; the huddled low mountains, gently swept by the late afternoon sun, cradle the calm waters of the ancient heart of Ullswater.

It is a cold clear bright wide open day; as he had hoped, from here in places the sun catches the surface of the lake so as to set it shimmering in a thousand places.

He looks out across the ancient waters. He knows this lake. He has slept upon its shores. He half-believes a great spirit or spirits might well reside here, in its depths. Indifferent. For a moment a thin shadow of shifting cloud shades the light. Dark thoughts press in upon him. The loss of John. The hostile response to his work so far. Money and the want of it. His wife Mary, the two children, a third child on the way. The relentless madman poised on the other side of the English Channel. Annette and Caroline.

He looks across at the ancient low mountains. Majestic? Yes. Indifferent? Perhaps. The faint shadow passes through; the soft light of the setting sun once more rolls a pale ochre glow over the shrugged slopes, rolls through the valley before him.

His breathing slows; he closes his eyes, lowers his head. He can hear a light breeze gently stir the trees in the forest below, feel its slight force upon his face. Somewhere close to him a bird sings a two-note song, asserts its place in the land.

He raises his head, opens his eyes. All is as it was, as it will be.

Time for the post-carriage and home.

*

Later the same day he is sitting on a padded bench in the White Lion in Patterdale, enjoying a pint of pale ale and resting his tired feet. The post-carriage is expected at any time. Outside the short November day has finally faded out.

A low fire is burning in the hearth at the far end of the long bar.

James Butler Esquire, landlord of this place, short, heavy, thick black curly hair now balding, a face full of doubtful laughter and life's creases, is talking loudly to a few other men who are stood around the bar.

"I tell you I can pull on this handle and provide all of you with a proper pint each and not move off this stool . . ."

The men laugh into his face, some shake their heads, curse lightly.

Jim Butler laughs and with a great dramatic gesture flaps out the damp off-white canvass beer-towel in front of his big belly.

"Gentlemen, please stand back and await your pleasure."

The men all crowd in around the bar, unsure if a trick is being played on them or not.

Jim reaches out to the shiny brass handle, and begins to pump the handle up and down, his thick forearm working furiously.

"Bloody hell, we can see how you've got in plenty of practice before now . . ."

Some of the men throw back their heads to laugh, nod, exchange sly glances; they understand the trade-off.

There is a loud gurgling noise, a fizz, a trickle, spots of foam.

Jim looks up from his work, smiling broadly

"Now then, watch this . . ."

Slowly the dark brown liquid begins to flow into the pint pot; all watch mesmerised. Soon enough the pot is full, and a pint of ale crowned with a fine frothy head is standing on the bar. The men are impressed; one or two begin to clap and murmur their quiet approval.

James Butler Esquire, landlord, beams in triumph at his audience.

"It's called a beer engine; they've had them down in London for a few years. Now I've got one – no more cellar steps barrels and buckets for me, lads, this is the future . . ."

He stops speaking. Behind the backs of the men in front of him, he can see through the wide windows that look out onto the main village road, narrow here, a crowd of people, some walking, some running, as they make their way across and along the road and head for the main door of the pub. There is a commotion, loud talking, some cheers. Everybody in the main room is now following his gaze.

"Summat's up . . ."

With an onrush of cold air, the main door is thrown back and the people push into the pub, all speaking at once, a hubbub, pushing right up to the main bar.

Jim holds up his arms.

"Stop now, calm down, what's all this then?"

A thick-set man in the front of the crowd shouts excitedly

"I'll tell you what it is! We're saved from Boney, Jim, we're saved from Boney! Tell 'em, Clem, tell 'em just as you told us!"

A tall well-made young man, strong flushed face, his hat held to his chest, looks at the landlord, looks around at all in the pub. There is a hush; he blurts the words out all at once.

"A great victory! He saw 'em off! He saw 'em off! The Spanish and French fleets all destroyed, broken up, our lads barely touched, Boniparty's turned away, he's goin after the Russians!"

Cheers go up in the pub, people turn to each other, hesitate, a movement, a new energy, they get to their feet, smile, eyes wide, clap each other on the back, start to hug each other.

The young man holds up his left arm. Again, a momentary silence in the room.

Now he speaks quietly, choking on the words; his head is lifted, his eyes shine.

"But they got him, they got him. They took him too. Admiral Nelson is dead, they took our leader with 'em, he's gone . . ."

All noise ceases.

All now look at each other, confused.

An old man sitting at the bar on a high wooden stool stands up. In one convulsive movement he tears his cloth cap from his head, throws it to the floor, curses, falls slowly to his knees, brings his hands up to his head, sobs, broken.

Nobody speaks.

The walking man has watched all of this in silence. Now he stands up, walks across to the old man who is still convulsed in sobs. He bends his knee at his side, places his right hand under the elbow of the old man and helps him back to his feet. He retrieves the cap and places it on the counter, taps the old man on the shoulder, turns in a shy way towards the crowd, nods, takes his old French frockcoat from its peg, walks out of the main door.

Outside the air is cold, sharp. He fastens the coat, walks a few paces to his right. Although he cannot now see them in the fading light, he knows that the mass of High Street stands behind him and, beyond the single row of little houses huddled into the hillside, broad shouldered Helvellyn rears up to his left; the high narrow mountain path through the Spikes hangs dangerous way up to his right. Ahead of him, the other side of Glenridding, if he takes the long valley road, the lake will lie before him once more, becalmed; no storms stir its silent banks. He nods to himself; yes, with good fortune he has many years to complete his work. He can see at an angle through the gap towards the long straight section of road in the direction of Glenridding. As he looks, he sees a yellow light; it flickers, hovers perhaps six feet above the ground, moves through the space he can see in the gap a quarter mile from him, then is lost behind a few scattered houses before the road's curve.

The news just heard. The felt heft of mountains. The cold clear night air. The brave warm glow from the tavern's windows which defies the early dark.

For a few moments he can hear no sound at all. The sudden sense of something beyond language. The mystery of it all.

The sound of hooves.

The lamp of the post-coach as it rounds the curve in the road.

wave

He stands at the window looking out over St Petersburg.

All is covered in snow; the thaw has barely started. Troikas and carriages skim along the main parade; the Neva and the canals remain frozen, though the early Spring is sufficiently advanced for the people to no longer venture out onto the ice. From where he stands, watching from the high closed window, all seems silent. People stutter or skip lightly along the streets, heavily wrapped up against the biting cold, all isolated in their thoughts, as they make for a meeting, a rendezvous, or home, places where they can again begin to talk, to discuss, to communicate, to tell each other how the world seems to be on this bitterly cold day in March.

He opens a window slightly to let in the cold air. He turns back to the room and looks again at the elegant Swiss clock mounted on the wall above the mantelpiece. It is ten minutes to ten o'clock in the morning. The room is not particularly large; the light oak parquet floor is carpeted with rich Persian rugs; a stout red mahogany table, highly polished, dominates the centre space. Arranged around the walls are tasteful paintings of weary, knowing, men, all with white hair and grey beards, each portrait ornately framed.

He moves to the top of the table, nervously glances again at the blackboard set up at its head as he does so. He gently lifts the hand-bell and rings it twice. The general chatter and bustle of his several scientist colleagues, dotted around the room, dies down. They turn towards him. He addresses them in the sudden quiet.

"Gentlemen, if you would care to join me at the apparatus, we should soon be able to start the experiment."

There is a move towards the top of the table; a semi-circle is formed around him as he stands before a mechanical and wooden construction. A metal rod attached to the wall is connected to the apparatus.

"To briefly explain what we should witness if the experiment proves to be a success."

He gestures towards the apparatus.

"My colleague Madame Kabrina is in a room approximately two

hundred and fifty yards away from where we stand here. In a few minutes, she will start to transmit a signal to this room. If the experiment is to succeed, we should begin to receive those signals using this apparatus, which includes a modified version of the coherer device produced by the Englishman, Sir Oliver Lodge. The coherer is connected to this rod, which we call an antenna, and to a separate circuit with a relay and battery which will operate this electric bell. The transmitted signal should turn on the coherer, the current from the battery will be applied to the relay, closing its contacts, which, in turn, will apply current to the electromagnet of the bell, pulling the arm over to ring the bell. My own invention allows the bell arm to spring back and tap the coherer, restoring it to its receptive state."

Polite applause flows gently around the room.

"For the experiment we will be using a modified version of Morse Code. A long ring of the bell will signify a dash; a short ring of the bell will signify a dot."

He turns to the man standing next to him.

"Mr President, if you will join me, I would like you to participate in this historic experiment."

The President of the Physical and Chemical Society of St Petersburg, a man of average height who has a large head covered in waves of white hair and a very white wavy beard, nods with good humour, smiling.

"Of course Popov, of course, only too happy to oblige . . ."

Popov hands the President a stick of chalk.

"If the experiment works, we will spell out a name on the blackboard, which will prove that it is possible to communicate over distances by means of Hertzian waves, otherwise known as electromagnetic waves and discovered by the late Mr Heinrich Hertz six years ago."

He glances over his shoulder at the clock on the wall behind him, even as it begins a clear, precise chime of the hour.

"So gentleman, it is ten o'clock. Let us begin."

All look at the apparatus. The chimes cease. There is no movement in the room; an occasional cough, a muffled shout from the street below.

Nothing is happening to the apparatus. It stands there, its polished wood gleams, its receiver stays silent. Popov does not move, shows no sign of agitation. Suddenly there is a hum in the coherer; the arm swings across to the bell, strikes it with short sharp stokes four times, each time returning to the coherer and tapping it too.

43

The president starts up, turns to the blackboard.

"That was four dots!"

He writes a large H on the board.

A pause. Then a hum, a swing of the arm to the bell.

"One dot!"

He writes the letter E on the board.

Now members of the audience look at each other, a murmur of excited voices passes through the room.

Now the apparatus is in full motion; a hum, the arm swings back and forth, more letters spelt out on the board. And so it continues. With each sequenced swing of the arm, there is now excitement, spontaneous applause in the room, because all can see whose name will be spelt out.

Soon enough, the President stands back from his handiwork. The words:

HEINRICH HERTZ

are clearly picked out on the blackboard.

Popov is now flushed, he beams with delight; everything has happened as he had anticipated. Distinguished men come up to him and slap him on the back. He shakes his head in wonder.

Sustained applause breaks out in the room. All feel a gentle sense of something bigger than their lives, of history, of lightness, as if they too have played their part in this scientific success, the proof of these Hertzian waves which might have such incalculable application in the future.

Popov holds up his arm, nods, pleased with the successful outcome.

"Gentlemen, I think all of us are witness to the success of this day. You will know from my paper last year that it is my hope that my apparatus will be applied to signal across great distances by electric vibrations of high frequency, as soon as a more powerful generator of such vibrations is invented."

He pauses, takes a sip of water, then looks around at his colleagues.

"I have one last issue that I must mention to all in the room. Clearly this experiment today has taken place under the auspices of the Russian Naval School, and as such, it is protected by necessary, confidential protocols of the Russian Government. Much as it pains me to say it, we are not at liberty to share what we have witnessed today with the wider world, indeed, with anybody outside this room. However, we will continue with our work, and one day no doubt the wider world will get to know what it is that we have witnessed in this room today."

There is more applause and a little more discussion. Then one by one, or in groups, the assembled men wander over to Popov, shake his hand, and then take their leave of the room.

Only Popov remains.

He goes over to the table and places a heavy red cloth over the apparatus. Then he turns and looks at the words written on the blackboard. He takes one step back, absorbs again the words spelt out:

HEINRICH HERTZ

Then he steps up to the blackboard and erases the words. He picks up the stick of chalk and writes:

ALEXANDR STEPANOVICH POPOV

He steps back again and looks at the blackboard. His chin comes down in quiet reflection; then he chuckles to himself in a good-natured way, steps back to the blackboard, erases the words he has written and, with a light step, goes out through the door.

Now there is no sound in the room.

*

Earlier the same day, another Aleksandr, a workman, curses loudly the moment he wakes up.

He is lying on a camp-bed in the kitchen of a farmhouse on an estate set in the small village of Melikhovo, south of Moscow. Here in the kitchen the ice still lies thick upon the inside of the window-frames; the few blankets that bind him to the old wooden cot do nothing to stop the cold chill that seems to seep into him; he drowsily pictures himself as a blue fish trapped in ice on the lake.

"Damn winter! It's time the full thaw came."

His smoky white breath twirls and floats out of his mouth even as he mutters the words. He braces himself, throws back the blankets and reaches for his heavy coat, sewn in many places with blue and green patches. For some reason he thinks of his mother; she always despaired for him when he was a child.

"Your problem, son-o-mine, is that you want to wear the coat before you kill the bear!"

So she has always told him; she is right, too. He is a lazy man, and he knows it. But now things have taken a turn for the better, things aren't so bad. He is finally in at the doctor's place, and he is not a bad kind, as these sorts of people go. He does not beat him, nor does he make impossible demands. Paint, chop wood, mend fences, see to the horses. Now, in mid-March, he prepares the paths so that the floods will be kept to a minimum when the full thaw comes. If he keeps out of the way of the doctor's old father, with his mad rants and foul temper, he might be able to make a go of it. If he plays his cards right, this might be a good number for a few years; he might even be able to save a few roubles.

Aleksandr is a tall man with a spare wiry frame and a still blonde beard peppered with grey. He is no longer a young man, and he has lost the hair from his temples, so that he imagines that he looks like a teacher.

He throws more wood into the tiny stove and reaches for the samovar. The sooner he drinks tea, the sooner he might get some warmth into his bones.

He thinks again of his mother. She is in bed since last week because she has a high temperature. Soon it might become a full-blown fever. What will happen to him if she dies? She is his rock, his ship-in-a-storm, his protector. For a moment he imagines his life without the old woman, and physically trembles.

Something needs to be done, and soon.

He looks out of the window, wipes the ice-obscured pane with his coat-sleeve as he does so. Several tiny rivulets of water run down the glass. Beyond the pane he can see the thick-piled snow stretch beyond the paddock fence as far as the pine forest a half-verst in the distance. He sees that the doctor is already up, and leaning against the fence; he looks away to the pine forest. He sees the doctor raise his arm and wave to some distant figure Alexandr cannot see over in the direction of the snow-snagged trees in the forest.

Aleksandr knows what he has to do. He will ask the doctor to attend to his mother. A tricky business, this . . . he has only been on the doctor's estate for a couple of weeks and he has no wish to be seen as a burden.

He makes up his mind. Now is a good time to ask, first thing, before work; he will take the doctor his first cup of tea from the samovar.

Outside on the porch all is calm. Here in the shelter of the timber buildings no wind blows; the cold lumpy whiteness spreads to the horizon on all sides. A strong sun throws a gentle morning light over the pond in front of the farmhouse. There is no human figure to be seen for miles around. All is isolated, cut off; there is no way to talk to the outside world during winter, unless somebody braves the roads to arrange a visit.

The man leaning over the fence thinks of Gavrilovich, the pistol shot, all heard off-stage, Dorn's command to Trigorin to take Irena away – does that work on a stage? Is that the right place to end it? Will Stanislavsky understand the tone of the moment? Can he expect ridicule? Should he go to Moscow himself? He runs his hands up and down his face, through his still wavy hair. He looks out over the mute white mass, across which here and there spin eerie part opaque whirls of snow, caught by a passing breeze out there in the open land; looks across to the distant frigid woodland; perhaps he thinks: Why do I wrestle with this nonsense? What is this minute by minute restlessness, this anxiety to explain what I have sensed and understood, but which is hidden to us? What is this profound reality just beyond our reach which in our multiple distractions we have contrived to fail to see? *How might I find a way to communicate what I wish to say before this relentless stupid disease kills me?*

As Alexandr approaches the man, the workman rehearses the right words in his mind. Silently he gets to within five paces and speaks up.

"Most Honoured Doctor, good morning! May I say a few words to you about my mother?"

But he gets no further; even before he can turn to face Aleksandr the man suddenly bends forward and begins to cough, a deep rasping noise that comes up from the depths of his lungs, a terrible *gggh gggh* sound that does not cease, it seems to tear this man's lungs apart, his face is purple, his body convulses at bizarre angles, his effort to regain his breath more desperate each time the insistent high-pitched short squeezed air is punched from his lungs.

It is like no other sound made on the face of the earth.

Aleksandr curses himself for stating his request so boldly, watches with pity as the man desperately pulls a white cloth from his pocket and holds it to his mouth as the terrible spasms continue to wrack his body, to jerk his upper body this way and that in the snowbound yard.

Slowly the coughing fit dies away and weakly the man recovers his breath. His breathing begins to return to something like a regular

47

rhythm. He returns the white cloth to his pocket, holds it away from his sight as he does so.

He turns and leans gently against the fence, waves his hand behind him towards Alexandr; a couple of minutes pass as he tries to recover some sense of equanimity

Now he turns back wearily to the workman. The greying black hair is brushed back from the temples, though now a thick lock has fallen aslant; a heavy half-beard, also greying; the eye-glasses are held by a green string fastened to the right arm. There is a momentary irritation in his lined yet still almost youthful face, the vivid red streaks along his forehead and cheekbones are just beginning to fade. But then he sees the fearful eyes of the farm-worker, the spare frame wrapped in the patchwork coat, the steaming mugs of tea held in each hand. The fine lines around his own still-watering eyes relax; through his own fear he smiles, reaches out for the proffered cup.

Thoughts of temperamental and newly-fond Lika, of his long story about the provinces, the fate of the play which he will soon post to Moscow, the new school buildings, the lambing ewes: all of that might wait for now.

One day he will sell this villa and move south, to the Crimea.

Just then there is a loud tearing noise followed by a dull splash. A huge slice of snow and ice slides, slips forward into the pond. Here in the country the new strong sun causes the snow to begin to thaw.

An unsettled smile crosses over his features.

Before him, the workman still watches him closely.

"So! We shall see at least one more spring in this place, Aleksandr!"

He smiles into the mystified, calculating eyes of the farm worker. He steps forward, takes the workman's arm and they begin to trudge back towards the house.

"So tell me all about this mother of yours . . ."

Together they walk back to the steps, go up to the porch and go through into the house.

Now the immense snow-bound landscape is silent but for a tiny sound; the *drip drip drip drip* of melting snow, which causes ever-wider ripples to spread out across the surface of the pond.

jj reads the evening paper

A man sits in a wicker chair on a small balcony outside a bedroom in a second floor apartment which looks out on to high built city streets. He has set the chair so that at one end of the street he can see, beyond the narrow canyon formed by the tall buildings on each side which lead down to it, a glimpse of the teeming sea port, lifting derricks and cranes, red and black funnels, off-white canvas sails of ships either berthed, coming into port or setting out into some unknown journey.

This sea port is known by some romantic diehards of the regime as the beating heart of the Austro-Hungarian Empire.

My name shall be hallowed yet.

The thought, though laced with a deep Jesuit irony, causes his assertive jaw to tilt upwards, which momentarily throws his corrected vision out beyond the port at the far end of the street into the wider stretches of the sea.

He senses that he is finally coming into his kingdom. One day he will say that to Nora: *I am coming into my kingdom!* His work makes progress in the world. His creative will shall prevail.

Trinket toes gaily pad a rat-a-tat beat; a soft air gently assails the room.

A young girl, perhaps six or seven years old, thick curly hair, one eye slightly aslant in her sensitive, pretty face, comes into the bedroom. She puts her head through the open window which looks out onto the balcony. She talks in Triestino dialect: *mama wants to know if he will be eating with them this evening.* He gently sends her away; *no, he will be going down to the Old Town, to the Quays.*

With a father's tenderness he watches his daughter's frail form patter out through the bedroom door.

After a few more moments he peers again through the window at the old clock on the wall.

Five minutes to six o'clock.

Two minutes later, he is walking at pace over a bridge towards the yellow quays, towards a favourite bar in the *Citta Vecchia*, a place

49

where none of his pupils, all taken from the elite of the city, are likely to be seen. Maybe he will see a couple of colleagues from the Revoltella. If not, then he shall spend time with his old friends, the waiters, and whoever else is prepared to talk to him, to listen to him. Ten years in this transit city: a crossroads of many currents. Life is looking up. He waves and taps his cane jauntily, moves with a jaunty air. His linguist's brain thrills to the different voices, as men and women saunter through the warm soft evening, released on Sunday from the need to earn their daily bread, speaking Triestino, Italian, Slav, German, other languages too, he can hear these sounds spill out of every doorway, come towards him, recede, move away. There is vibrancy in the air; he anticipates the first glass with relish.

Ahead of him, a small crowd has gathered. A newsboy shouts something, repeating it, a rhythmic beat: there is mild commotion in the crowd around the boy.

Now he can hear the boy clearly:

"Assassination! Special edition! Read about it here!"

He pauses to peer at the billboard:

ASSASSINATED!
ARCHDUKE FRANZ FERDINAND IS DEAD.
SOPHIE DIES WITH HIM.
READ LAST WORDS HERE.
LEADERS TO HOLD CRISIS TALKS.

He hands across the coin and places the folded-up newspaper under his arm. With agility he moves away; his shoulder inadvertently comes together with the shoulder of a woman making her way to the vendor.

"Ah, forgive me!"

"No, no, forgive me, please!"

*

He sits alone in the *Cisterna*; he has been warmly welcomed by lean Giacomo and full-bodied Stefania (*"bellissima!"*), two youngish *triestinos* who run this place with a smile and a shrug. They have known him since he first came here, still boyish, with his sure plan to change the world in his own image. They like this Irish *professore*, with his strange ways, his talk of Aquinas and art, his weak inquisitive eyes, his sharp sceptical humour, his mischief, his generosity and, on the nights of near complete abandon, his loose-legged dances, his fine light tenor voice.

He has been happily led into temptation here; a carafe of *Fendant*, half-full, sits on the table in front of him. He turns his attention to the report of the assassination. He reads for the first time Franz Ferdinand's reported last words. He stops, checks himself, reads the words again. He looks up from the table, staring out of the open-fronted bar, as if he is in some other place. He looks back to the report. No sign of emotion shows on his face.

    "*. . . Sopherl! Sopherl! Sterbe nicht! . . . Bleibe am Leben für unsere Kinde! –*"

He takes off his wire-framed lenses, wipes them, looks out to the teeming streets as he does so, though still he seems to be in some other place. His eyes are blue, large. German, Triestino, English words echo in his mind.

    "*. . . Sophie, Sophie, don't die! . . . Stay alive for our children! –*"

Out on the pavements of Trieste he can see now only blurred images, can hear the triestino germanic slavonic italian voices of many strangers young and old, can sense the throbbing energy of life in many voices many strangers as if in this Babel all the nations of the world speak all the languages of the world, as they surge back and forth over the teeming city pavements, flow over the bridges of Trieste, as they move, march, sway, dodge, hurry through the warm evening sun, as they turn to talk to each other, to smile, profess, cajole, wheedle, argue, utter oaths, explode into laughter. Others with their heads down, worried by thoughts of what is to come, scurry home, alone.

A series of loud shouts, a whistle; still more sonorous bright laughter goes up from a squad of young men somewhere nearby, goes up . . . up . . . illuminates the evening air for a few brief moments before it fades away.

For a moment there is no sound, a strange lull.

A church bell sounds the hour.

He blinks again, replaces the lenses.

An electric tram careers past, shuddering clank of metal...

A beautifully made well-muscled chestnut horse stood between the shafts of a cart rears up . . . skits about . . . unsettled . . .

Deliver us.

51

fall

WRITERS DEMAND TO BE HEARD!

Guest Speaker: Herr Thomas Mann
NEUES WALDHOTEL,
AROSA
3 P.M FRIDAY
17 MARCH, 1933

The atmosphere in the room was one of general gaiety, almost as if we had been invited to a ball and the music was about to start.

In truth, Germany had taken the final turn about that time. It had begun with the torching of the Reichstag a few weeks previously, the new regime peddling some story of a communist plot, and had moved on to the round-ups and state executions. I had daily witnessed brown-shirt thugs heaving their beer-bellies about to molest innocent people going about their daily work; slowly we all had begun to realise that something new had been released into our lives, something gross, barbaric, as if the worse fools you might avoid on a city street, those bastards full of their own infantile certainties, had been given licence to beat you up. Now others who had witnessed these things, who had seen these things and knew that they would be next on the list, they had begun to pour out of Germany, and even the main speaker that day, Thomas Mann, had not returned to Munich from a lecture tour and was now here in our midst in Arosa, and would be addressing us all.

How I came to be in that place amongst the high mountains at that time is a long story, too long; but I can give you the immediate reason: a woman. God knows, the intervening ten years have aged beyond our years those of us who have remained in Germany in our futile attempt to resist the terror; but at that time I suppose I was a restless young man, agitated, trying to make coherent sense of it all and failing miserably. I had spent a few years in the late 'twenties hanging around in Berlin with Dix and Grotz, all that New Realism stuff; but it had grown stale for me. Utilitarianism, Americanism, live, work, make money, screw, get screwed or be screwed, one way or the other, all of that cynical exploration of the so-called true motivations of disinterested people. The trench has marked those two men, Dix and Grotz, for life. As I saw it then, there was something missing in that way of seeing the world. Those shadows moving about in the dark, the anything goes excess born out of the national humiliation as we all sank to the bottom of the trough. Not for me, not any of that.

So I had moved on to Munich, tied my flag for a time to the old Blue Rider school. At least here was something more, maybe, than the sordid New Realism reality. Munich nightlife had held me in its grip; its strange underworld had a crazy draw for me; I could see a recognisable version of myself up there on those sleazy stages amidst the smoke and decadence and debris of life. In one of those dens I had met Lena. We had understood each other from the first drink, or so I thought. For a few weeks we believed ourselves to be in love; I felt like a beggar who had stumbled upon a secret horde, a king's treasure.

One night we were sitting in the *Peppermill* review; between acts I was telling Lena about an incident I had seen that day. She looked directly into my eyes as I spoke:

"Some of the fat clowns were giving an old man a bad time in the street. I can see the old man's face; thin, lined, etched even; I remember deep folds of skin, ruts, ran down the length of his face on either side, from below each eye to his jaw-line. He had been wheeling an old wooden barrow, wheels with spokes missing, loaded with bits and pieces, trinkets, little more than rubbish. All of us watching, we all knew that barrow was his only means of survival. When they started in on him, he barely protested – he knew already how things would go. Then they knocked off his skullcap. As he bent down to pick it up, they had kicked him, sent him sprawling...."

Lena looked at me with those wide-set green eyes of hers, wild with more than a hint of cold cruelty at each corner, or so it seemed to me:

"And what did you do?"

"I wanted to stove their faces in. One of the thugs started to lean his fat belly onto the edge of the barrow, tried to lift the edge of the wooden rim, so that each time he stood back up the wheel on that side of the barrow lifted a little further off the road.

"'Uppp it goes...'"

"Now the other clowns joined in, laughing

"'Uppp it goes...Uppp and...over it goes!'"

"The barrow tipped over, sending all of the old man's precious stock, this rubbish collection of trash, spilling over the pavement. Those bastards were bent in half by their laughter"

"So what did you do?"

"We all stood there. Some jokers in the crowd cheered. Most were silent. We all waited...I was waiting for somebody older than me to step in, to make the first move, to stop this disgrace happening. But nobody moved. Apart from the jeerers, we all stood there in silence."

She looked away to the counter, glanced at herself briefly in the mirror which ran the length of the bar, pushed stray hair off her brow.

"So what happened?"

"Nothing happened. The Brownshirts slapped each other on the shoulder, laughing, then kicked the old man's trinkets around the street, before they walked away, still laughing. We lifted him to his feet. A few of us helped him to pick up what was left..."

"Such people sicken me."

I looked back into her steady mocking eyes. I wasn't sure which people she was referring to.

"Yes, these Brownshirts and the SA need sorting out."

Again the steady gaze.

"I did not mean them. You cannot save what has always been lost. I meant the people who stood there in the crowd, doing nothing."

A pause.

"It takes a brave man to go against these people now. They even have the law in their pocket these days..."

"Let me tell you something about that crowd. Some of them are enjoying the spectacle. Some of them are glad it's not them taking a kicking. Some of them want to join in; they feel they've been kicked around themselves, they think it's time somebody else took a good kicking...."

"Oh? And how do you know that?"

"It's clear! Open your eyes, you fool! Look at the election results, these people are half in love with the brutes, they see themselves striding the streets, powerful, shoving people out of their way. They should be taught how to think properly, by whatever means at hand...."

I looked at her again. I had heard this mantra several times in recent days, and each time it caused my teeth to grind in my mouth. I'd had enough of these all-knowing assertions. I bit back:

"You know, these people have been battered for years; the mark worthless, the repayments, the national humiliation, the unemployment.... and now you and your kind presume to know what they think, and demand how they must think...it seems to me it takes real arrogance to presume to know what somebody is thinking, to instruct people what they are to think...you know your problem? You have no real faith in humanity; at root you need everybody to feel as you feel, think as you think, as your friends feel and think..."

She looked at me once more, delicate muscles taut in her aristo face, now shadowed; the lines around her eyes had hardened:

"And you Klaus? Perhaps you are more like those people in the crowd than I thought. What do you think of your fellow man? Where do you stand?

"Me? This is not about me...though I think life is a thousand times more complicated than you say..."

"Yes, let's take your own example. There you stand, a big strong man, in your prime. Yet when those bullies kicked the old man, you stood there, like some impotent unstrung puppet, waiting for somebody to act, to yank your strings..."

She nodded to herself, looked away from me, glanced around the busy room.

"You know, as I imagine you standing there in that watching silent crowd, it strikes me as a pathetic sight...that you are in fact a pathetic man, when the hard questions come calling... "

She stubbed out her cigarette, smiled politely at me in a distant way, dismissed me finally with her eyes, got up from the bar stool, walked out of my life.

Over the next few days, I could not get what she had said out of my mind, day or night.

I needed a change; I decided to get away from the fetid atmosphere of Munich.

I had begun to look towards those places where I knew artists and thinkers were likely to be found – the same impulse which had first taken me to Berlin - and this little Swiss spa town up amongst the mountains had begun to gain that reputation; I knew of its connections with the work of Thomas Mann and just at that time it had also started to become something of a staging post for the new exiles; these people had begun to trickle into Arosa on a daily basis, taking in its clean air, all like me taking the single gauge railway winding up from Chur to the high ground beyond the Untersee.

So when, on the third day, I spotted the advertisement for this event it was like manna from heaven to me, stricken as I then was by the lure of artists and the mystique they seemed to carry with them.

And now I found myself in the very room in which the great man was to make his appearance.

A makeshift platform had been set up at the head of the old dining room of the *Neues Waldhotel*. This was a long narrow hall boasting vaulted arches at the entrance, with wood panelling set at half-height on the otherwise white-painted walls which had various interwoven Celtic designs painted onto their surface. Brass chandeliers hung from the ceiling, from which were suspended cream globes. Various doors at the top of the hall led out to the outside terrace. Chairs had been set out on either side of a centre aisle. The narrow width of the hall in relation to its length and high ceilings created a feeling of being hemmed in on each side, oppressed, partially relieved by the sunlight streaming in from the terrace behind the speaker's platform. This platform was no more than a few pallets quickly thrown together and covered with cloth sheets, upon which had been placed several tables laid side by side, also covered in cream cloth; most of the speakers already sat at these tables.

As I say, the room was gripped by a sense of lightness, almost as of a feast-day, as if those in the room had temporarily been given time off from their daily lives.

Now a door to my left opened with a flourish, and, seated as I was in the third row, in which there were still a few empty chairs out of deference to the sheer weight of the occasion, I caught my first good sight of the writer; close-cropped hair at the back and sides, greying hair brushed from a proud tensed forehead, close deep-set eyes beneath thick eyebrows, the surprisingly patchy, close-clipped black and grey Prussian moustache decorating the top lip, the large nose, prominent ears.

Please understand me; this man was something like a demi-god to me at that time. Not him in his person, his physical self, his everyday strengths and weaknesses, his refined sensibilities, nor too his all too-human flaws and foibles which we all share. None of that held my attention for more than a moment. It was the patience and sheer endurance embedded in his work, and emerging from the work the series of noble, flawed human figures, as if struck free from the hardest marble blow by blow - this discipline and application evident in his contribution to the progress of humanity – it was all of this which held me in thrall.

As he sat down, I immediately noticed a quickness in his movements, if only of his eyes, or in the way in which he looked up at the audience, or at a co-speaker, or took his chair, as if the thought to act in that way had never previously occurred to him before that very moment.

The Chairman stood up.

"Ladies and Gentlemen, welcome to our event this afternoon. As you can see, we are delighted to welcome a very special guest to our humble proceedings..."

Spontaneous applause burst out in the hall. Thomas Mann lifted his hand in acknowledgement. As this was happening, for some reason I felt struck by a sudden sense of claustrophobia and happened to glance behind me to see if the heavy main doors had been closed. I noticed three well-groomed young men push through the closing doors and enter the hall. Two of them found seats set wide apart at the back of the hall. The other man, wearing a black leather jacket, black pressed trousers and holding an attaché case, strode up the centre aisle, looked about him, pushed his way along the row in which I sat and took a vacant chair a couple of seats away from my own. He ignored my amiable look of greeting as he did so.

The Chairman smiled, also raised his hand and continued:

"...thank you thank you. A few necessary preliminaries, good house-keeping as it were..."

He spoke of the usual formalities.

"Now the order of the event will be as follows. Each of our writers will be invited to stand and speak to the floor, and, if they so choose, to read from their latest work. At the end, we shall ask Herr Mann to address us directly. Thank you..."

Again polite applause.

Several speakers took to the floor in their turn. There was at least one sorrowful Werther, and a set of disguised Brunhildes and Siegfrieds returning with a revived Wotan and weeping over the desecrated land, and so on and so forth. The main guest seemed to take it all in good spirit, even if occasionally drumming his fingers on the table-top in an unguarded moment.

"And now, to finally round off our list of writers before we get to the main event of the evening, I call upon our own Herr Taschenspieler who has thought it best, in the ...err...circumstances, to return to us from Germany. He will regale us with a few carefully chosen words and...I think one of your stories?"

There was a note of doubt in the voice of the host as he said this, whilst looking at Herr Taschenspieler, who promptly nodded his assent and stood up. He held a manuscript in his left hand. This fellow seemed distant, buttoned up, reserved to the point of extreme shyness; his movements stiff, abrupt, almost rehearsed. My first impression was of a Prussian count of the old school, junker class, gone badly to seed; he was comically overdressed in a three-piece tweed suit, dress shirt and bow-tie, though all there could see that his clothes were threadbare. He gave a curt bow to the audience and it was clear he wished to address us, to unburden himself before the master, after which he would read aloud his manuscript to the room. He spoke in a strong though subdued voice. He made no introduction, just began to speak in such simple guileless language, so completely free from self-protecting irony that I made a point of noting some of his words at the time;

"My present turmoil in these terrible times visited upon us has come as a surprise even to me, long accustomed to the anxieties and demons that seem to be so much a part of the creative burden. I know more than most of the terrible impact of the creative impulse on the vitality of the human spirit!"

As he spoke, I noticed Thomas Mann's eyelids flicker momentarily before he again stared ahead of him, his eyes fixed upon the white tablecloth.

"To speak plainly, it seems to me in my current state of exile that to be an artist equates to an admission of the knowledge of the incurable loneliness of the human soul on its journey through this life, as a traveller crosses a stone bridge at night into a new country, a new territory of light and dark fraught with ambivalence and the doubleness of all things. ..."

At these words Thomas Mann raised his chin, frowning, and turned his head a fraction towards the speaker; his eyes flicked across and upwards at Taschenspieler with another of those strange quick movements, before settling back on the table-top. He listened intently to the words spoken.

"Yet out of this chaos comes order, for those strong enough to walk this path. And so the creative artist returns, must return, must come back from this other place to the real world, especially now in the dark realities that unfold before us, to the world of men and women and flesh and blood and emotions, to the world of love and hate, of life, bearing gifts and treasures, laments and dire warnings...."

Thomas Mann stared at the table. He briefly brought his hand to his forehead, winced.

"For if this loneliness is our lot, how precious, how fragile, is our time we spend together in this life, sharing its joys and terrors, its fears and hopes? This, it seems to me, is the nub of it; this is my vocation as artist, and I am no more capable of resisting this unbidden need to communicate my experience through my art than I am of resisting the need to breathe."

Now the fingers of Thomas Mann drummed the table again.

Taschenspieler began to read his script; I have no note of the story, it made no impression upon me of any kind. Thomas Mann stared harder at the table. As the words poured from the enraptured speaker, I saw our esteemed guest blink several times. I could swear that a look of the deepest boredom, perhaps anger, even contempt, passed through his features, though he tried to disguise it. The great writer closed his eyes; a pulse began to beat in his temple - it seemed to me he would be anywhere else in the world than sitting at that table listening to friend Taschenspieler's story.

As the strangely dressed fellow read aloud, I noticed the young man to my left calmly making note after note. Taschenspieler concluded; his reading was politely received by the audience. I saw that Thomas Mann barely stirred, other than to flick a speck of dust from the table-cloth before him.

Now the guest speaker himself was introduced in a long rambling speech by the Chairman:

"...of our national treasure that is Buddenbrooks"..."the haunting tale of the cholera and the obsession"..."the great opus set in a sanatorium, indeed perhaps partly in a transposed version of this very room"..."the final ascent of Olympus and the offering of the ultimate garland..."

To all of which the great writer made appropriate demurring movements and short protestations as the fellow built his stumbling oratory to some sort of limp crescendo.

Amidst more applause Thomas Mann stood up and began to address the floor. Barely middle height and of slight frame, his voice was a low tenor; trained, modulated to an agreeable pitch. He spoke slowly, in fact so slowly it now seems strange to me when I recall it, with precision and deliberation. It seemed to me he spoke under some great burden. I made a note of some of what he said, trying to capture to the best of my ability the spirit of the man.

"You will forgive me, but in my present position I feel more than ever the need to reach out to fellow cousins-in-spirit such as yourselves, and even more so to those fellow spirits who know the German soul. I trust that here, amongst such kindred spirits, I too might begin to unburden myself."

As he said this he looked along the table at Taschenspieler, and seemed to nod towards him. I saw the poor deluded man's chest visibly swell with pride as he acknowledged the compliment. Thomas Mann's subtlety was not lost on many in the audience around me, who smiled secretly to themselves at this not ungenerous cruelty as the laureate continued:

"My own journey to this place has been eventful. I had presented a version of my Wagner essay in lecture form on tenth February at the University in Munich, leaving immediately for Amsterdam, Brussels and Paris to continue the wider Wagner celebrations. We came here to Arosa for a period of recuperation. In light of events, there has been no such rest. Whilst here, well-intentioned friends have made clear to me that it is not wise for me to return to Munich; we had counted on the Bavaria elections and the strength of the Catholic League there; the election outcome is a disaster, for me and for my country. I fear for the consequences.

"Much else of course has occurred in the intervening weeks. It began with the destruction of the Reichstag – are we to believe that the culprit was one communist plotter acting alone? So they have passed the Fire Decree. And now they prepare the so-called Enabling Act – will von Hindenburg and von Papen hand complete control of the legislature to our mighty new Chancellor? It appears highly likely. I hear the horrors continue almost daily; all civilised values are disintegrating by the day. The price my country will pay for such folly is incalculable.

"Following these terrible events, I remain out of Germany. Until now as a proud German, a German writer, it has been possible to speak, to write, to fight in this way for truth. Freedom existed. There was none of this ugly immorality of repression we see in the streets of Munich and elsewhere. We Germans have been fools to allow it to happen, and I fear that in the years to come we will despair at what we have done, what we have unleashed."

For a moment he paused, lost in some thought. Then he gestured towards the front row of the audience:

"Good people, I would if I may draw your attention to my wife Katia, who is here this evening."

A slight-built woman stood up and raised her hand. A warm burst of applause swept through the hall. Her husband continued:

"I stand here before you accused of "intellectual high treason", of "pacifistic excesses". Today we start out together on a new life, my wife and I, a new basis for our existence, out of the Germany we knew and loved. I go into this exile with some apprehension. I am no longer a young man. However, whatever is to come, I trust my creative temperament will allow me the flexibility in life to survive such a new beginning, and as long as I have my brave wife beside me I am afraid of nothing."

With that, the great man sat down, to be met by rapt applause from the floor.

When this finally petered out, the chairman again got to his feet, and began to thank the guest speaker. Just then, the fellow next to me stood up. His high cheekbones had reddened; he held his notebook in his right hand.

'Herr Mann, one moment please, if I may...'

All in the room looked around to see who was speaking. The fellow spoke out in a ringing voice, confident.

"Herr Mann, I had the pleasure to attend your Wagner reading in Munich last month. Such subtlety, such finesse; such heights! Surely this was one great man in spiritual dialogue with another?"

Thomas Mann looked at the speaker closely. After a short pause he acknowledged the compliment gracefully. Gentle applause drifted around the room.

The speaker lifted his notebook;

"If I might quote briefly...

"'Let us be content to reverence Wagner's work as a mighty and manifold phenomenon of German and western culture, which will always act as the profoundest stimulus to art and knowledge.'"

The cocksure young man, high cheekbones now glowing, a lock of hair falling over his smooth forehead, looked around at the audience.

"I ask all here: Can there be a more precise statement of the importance of the divine German soul of the author of the Ring?"

Again polite applause showered the room. The Chairman smiled benignly; Thomas Mann continued to stare hard at the speaker.

"But then, what is this we come upon?"

Again, he raised the notebook and quoted:

"'...this man of the people, who all his life long and with all of his heart repudiated power and money, violence and war...'"

"I ask you, is this a true reading of the Aryan soul of our mighty German artist? And then we read this:

"'...such a man no retrograde spirit may claim for its own, he belongs to that will which is directed to the future.'"

The peacock paused; he looked around the room as all there hung on his words. The hall was silent under his rising voice.

"What can our famous author mean by these words? To which 'retrograde spirit' does he refer? Does he doubt our new Chancellor? And now, in this very room, he is condemned by his own words. He seems to doubt the truth of our great movement, our movement which even now takes great strides towards establishing the new Reich, the great future which even now hoves into clear sight for our Fatherland..."

Those seated near me began to throw glances at each other. The smile slowly faded from the face of the Chairman. Thomas Mann lowered his head, stared hard at the cream cloth on the table. I saw the local writer, Taschenspieler, produce a pair of rimless eyeglasses and stare hard at the young man. The speaker pressed on, his voice risen an octave:

"We must now ask ourselves; are these really the words of a true German?"

Thomas Mann raised his arms in a gesture of exasperation. One or two shouts came from around the room.

"Yes, a true German!"

"Let nobody here say otherwise...!"

"Your kind are not wanted here..."

The fellow's eyes, now protruding from the flushed face, turned back to the great man. He raised his arm, pointed his finger, pronounced his verdict in a shrill high voice:

"We have looked into you, Mann. We know about you. There are rumours about you and your reputation....for example your tainted non-Aryan blood on your mulatto mother's side..."

A wave of indignation mixed with shock rippled across the room.

"This is an outrage"

"...shame on you..."

"...what gives you the right...?"

One or two people in the audience had already begun to move quietly towards the exit door; they had not anticipated this ugly turn of mood, had felt it, had instantly recoiled from it.

From the back of the room suddenly came another shout:

"An effeminate man too, that's what they say in Munich..."

And again from the opposite side of the room, back and forth, amidst cries of protest:

"Some of those who know him, they say he adores boys of a certain age, just like von Aschenbach, yes, that's what they say in Munich..."

Again from the opposite side of the room:

"Yes, it is von Aschenbach we see in the flesh, in this room, this very day..."

"Truly a degenerate man..."

"Think of it. What a life his poor wife must lead...but then the wife too, oh yes, we know all about her..."

Thomas Mann took a couple of steps backwards, turned sideways on to the audience, as if for a moment he might run from the room out onto the Terrace. A look of naked vulnerability came into his face. His anxious eyes searched for Katia; she immediately stood up and moved across to his side. As she did so, Thomas Mann again raised his arms in protest to the Chairman, said something we could not hear, but the man looked blankly to his left, to his right, overwhelmed by the immediacy of the changed tone...now the sound of raised voices, hubbub, staccato shouts, unrest, a scuffle at the back of the hall, movement in front of me, falling chairs...an unsettled energy caused people to jerk about in their chairs, to stand up, to look about them...

Somebody near to my right ear shouted:

"You have no place here...Go back to Hell, you Nazi bastards..."

But now the fascist appeared as if transformed: his eyes bulged from his head, the red face was contorted; words were spat out as he shouted amidst a rising frenzy as other people tried to shout him down, to curse, to kick away their chairs:

"Yes we see there your wife, Frau Mann, born Pringsheim... the Jewish strain is in her, she is of tainted blood..."

"Shut your filthy mouth..."

"You Nazi spawn...get back to the hole you crawled out of..."

My heart pounded, blood thumped through my veins...already I knew that whatever was to unfold in this room, it could not be stopped now. I saw Frau Mann's jaw lift, her mouth and eyes fill with disdain at the psychotic words. Even in my agitated state, it occurred to me that of the two of them stood there, the great writer and his wife, it was the woman at that moment who was the stronger spirit in action, even as the demon pointed again at Thomas Mann, screamed out his brute inhuman credo amidst cries of anguish and fury:

"Thomas Mann, you have consorted with the Jewish strain, you have lain with them, you have produced a brood with them and your soul is forever lost...you have abdicated your privileged position in the new Reich, you are no true German, you have no place..."

So now the fiend was finally fully revealed, as if the human husk had fallen away to reveal this monster amongst us.

My heart pounded in my head, my blood raced...my body moved three steps to my left and on the third step I drove my right fist full into the face of this demon. I connected flush with bone and cartilage in the centre of its face and I saw the burst flesh spread out over its skull and I felt warm deep red blood splash out over my face and bare arm and over the fallen chairs now scattered across the floor around us.

For perhaps five seconds I felt a sense of purest exaltation and I smiled. The transfer of weight from left leg to right, the balance of my body, the pivot of the right arm, the sheer force of the leveraged blow, the connection...the perfect coherence of body and mind, the sudden silence after the ugly words...

The body had fallen back over chairs, half-propped up by wide-spread arms, eyelids wide open. I looked into the dislocated eyes rolling in their sockets, the lolling tongue lying flat on the white teeth of the open mouth amidst the blood, saw that his senses were splayed; as he lay there, odd guttural noises began to escape from his throat and the swollen bitten tongue moved whilst the head jerked in a macabre spasm and I knew in his scattered mind he continued to hurl his vile hatred out into the room; a sudden nausea filled my guts, causing my knees, unseen, to sag. Once, I thought, once, deep within this broken husk there must have been a human being, a person who had made choices, one who had once perhaps had hope of a different path...I looked at my swollen knuckles, bewildered. In moments I had become *like him*.

Then the shame swept through me.

*

I sit at my desk. I make this record of the events of that day. The blue octavo notebook I had with me that day lies next to my right hand. So too does a volume of the works of Thomas Mann.

I wait for the frenzied *thud thud thud* on the main door to my apartment.

Several of the writers in the audience that day chose to return to Germany. I see their faces, with so many others, each time I think of the sealed trains in the night which never return. Just last week I was contacted by Uti, the daughter of my good friend Taschenspieler, who told me her kind, gentle father had gone that way.

After the fracas that day I was interrogated by the security police. They were convinced I was the ring-leader of the fascists. I was locked up in a cell overnight.

During the night I felt as if the stone floor of the cell might give way beneath me and I would fall headlong into God knows what untethered place might exist below. I have never known, now will never know, another night like it; it was as if my mind was all but unhinged by the trauma, the frenzy of the day just gone. The fascist had sung the evil song of his tribe; I had cut short his song. In doing so, for a moment I felt as if I had shared something with this creature. The few truths I had pulled together up to that point in my life seemed to fall away, to dissolve. What was I? What motivated me? What was this brute I had become in moments? Was this what I was? So many tribes, so many savage songs, so much division and hate. One fallen tribe splintered into a million fragments? I found myself trying to recall the already half-forgotten words of the local writer, Taschenspieler, of all people...what had he said? They had not taken my notebook:

'...as a traveller crosses a stone bridge at night into a new country, a new territory of light and dark fraught with ambivalence and the doubleness of all things....'

In the unsettled dawn of a grey new day I held fast to a hard-won intuitive hope; move towards the light, never lose sight of the light.

In late morning they set me free. The Chairman had finally come into the gendarmerie and 'set the record straight', as they said. They told me the fascists had been patched up, driven down the mountain by the Federal Guard and taken back to the border; warned never to return. Thomas Mann they said had wanted to play no visible part in the aftermath of the episode; my last sight of him had been to see him bundled out of the hall by the top exit into the sun-filled terrace as I was led out of the main entrance in handcuffs; he and his wife had left Arosa later the same day. I hoped he had spoken up for me.

I walked out into the clean, free, mountain air. Old fellow Taschenspieler had been there to meet me, to make sure I was unharmed. Over time we had become friends.

Ah! So clean and free did the mountain air feel to me that day! To be able to feel it now for just one more moment upon my face! I have fought against the terror, against the dark, with my every breath since I walked out into that bright fresh Spring day ten years ago.

I sit at my desk. There is no hope of escape. They have been watching the sole exit for three days now. Soon I will hear the main entrance to my apartment burst open in the hallway below, will hear the barked orders, the well-drilled crunch of disciplined boots on the stone steps leading up to my door; then I must suffer the cruel pantomime of stupid unconscious men as they scream and obey their regular orders.

My hope, born in that cell in Arosa, has sustained me; despite all I have witnessed since that day, my hope has grown. For some reason it is not the polished professional eloquence or delightful artifice and studied nuance to be found in the work of Thomas Mann which I seek at this moment. What words had old Taschi used? I pick up the battered blue octavo notebook:

"...how precious, how fragile, is our time we spend together in this life, sharing its joys and terrors, its hopes and fears?"

I feel the full naivety, the not-knowingness of these words. All of it. Yet for some reason, in this moment, it is the simple ragged sincerity of these words I have reached for now.

Through ten thousand tiny portals in the dark, the light teems through, teems through.

I believe in that light.

king of the sun

At one forty-five pm Eastern and two forty-five am JST, a flight of military aircraft takes off from North Field, Tinian in the Mariana Islands. Six hours later and at just over 31,000 feet they are above their target. On board are members of the 509th Composite Unit of the United States Army Air Force; the lead aeroplane, the one with the payload, is named after the mother of its pilot. During the flight, the bomb has been primed. One hour previously the aircraft Straight Flush (task: weather reconnaissance; call sign: Dimples 85) has flown over the target and given the message,

"Cloud cover less than 3/10th at all altitudes. Advice: bomb primary"

*

He is tall, heavy, more densely-packed than one might expect for a man of his age. His hair is white, combed back and still wet, his head large, even in proportion to his giant body, his face is reddish-pink, newly bathed. He sits there swathed in an expensive white dressing gown, prim in his favourite chair in his den at the back of the house overlooking the garden.

A night bird booms mournfully in the high foliage.

All is good. It is nine o'clock on a warm and beautiful evening in early August in Hartford, Connecticut.

He is looking at the brown moon, brown bird, through the open windows, staring at it there in its momentarily precise and correct place over the right shoulder of the weathered Buddha from Ceylon, which even now basks in the heat of this Connecticut summer. Earlier, his wife had set out several vases brimming with red roses which now adorn the bedside table, the window sill, the antique Parisian cabinet which stands over in the far side of the room. His mild protests had been brusquely disregarded as she tripped about him in her hyper-tense, tiny-footed manner, stating plainly,

". . . This room needs colour and life."

The sweet musty smell of full blooming flower fills his nose as he sits here contemplating the brown moon, brown bird.

She has now retired for the night to her side of the house.

Alone, he has enjoyed a couple of glasses of very good Moselle. He rises from the chair slowly and, as if he treads a familiar path, almost absent-mindedly goes to each flower-bedecked vase and lifts it, carries it out of his bedroom, lines them all up along the wall on the far side of the landing, then returns to his cave.

He moves well and has enjoyed the vintage wine. Like some old firecat in his lair, he almost swaggers as he pours his large frame deliberately through each movement as he returns to his desk; there is even the hint of a dance step, a swerve to the left, a swerve to the right, his right hand held lightly against his chest, dressed in his *robe roi soleil,* in his *foyer,* a cha-cha coo-coo chi-chi so-so rocking kind of a movement.

He will return the vases before she rises tomorrow morning.

Here, in his den, his mind slowly releases the daily turmoil. He remains vaguely aware of the eight files coming to a head - even though all have been farmed out to outside counsel, he will have to travel to at least two hearings, may well attend one or two of the settlement negotiations himself. Marble Cake the black and white pigeon and his daily fluttery visitations, Kraft's Limberger Spread, Turgeniev and Valery are all much in his thoughts, so too is the digging back to his Dutch-German ancestors. His eyes cloud; perhaps he is thinking of those ultimatums from Truman over the radio – clearly the next, probably final, phase is in play.

He looks again at the brown moon. He already muses of celestial rendezvous and red fragrances squeezed from the stump of summer . . .

*

"Cloud cover less than 3/10th at all altitudes. Advice: bomb primary"
Thirty minutes previously, the safety devices have been removed.

The release at 08:15 (Hiroshima time) goes as planned, and Little Boy's payload of about 64 kg (141 lb) of uranium-235 takes 44.4 seconds to fall from the aircraft flying at about 31,000 feet (9,400 m) to a detonation height of about 1,900 feet (580 m) above the city. Enola Gay (task: weapons delivery; call sign: Dimples 82) travels 11.5 miles (18.5 km) before it feels the shock waves from the blast.

The Great Artiste (task: blast measurement; call sign: Dimples 89) is the last Flying Fortress to leave the scene.

He does not, will never, drive an automobile. He walks in a stately, deliberate manner, memorable, dignified. There is, perhaps, a trace of the bully in his too-conscious step. He wears a curiously old-fashioned felt hat to protect his head from the early morning heat of the sun. He has left the house in something of a hurry; he wants to walk the three or four miles to reach the Hartford before nine and he is always on time. A rolled up copy of the *Hartford Courant* is tucked away into the left pocket of the habitual steel-grey suit jacket which he wears like unadorned armour plate; he suffers in silence the heat of the sun.

He walks for a purpose. Words are running through his mind. He turns into Asylum Avenue, pauses. He reaches into the inside pocket of the jacket, finds a blank envelope, scribbles words quickly, nods, places the paper back into the same pocket as the *Courant.*

Before him he can now see the fine upright pillars of the Company and to the right of those pillars on the first floor, his office in the Hartford Accident and Indemnity wing. He mounts the eleven steps up to the portico on which the pillars stand with the same deliberate, measured, dignified stride.

*

The morning has been spent with the files. Stacks of them had been brought in on the stroke of nine. He picks each one up in turn, reads it, makes a note, either throws it absent-mindedly to the left-hand side of the office floor, or if more of his attention is needed, asks Miss Flynn to come in, quotes the file number, recites the address of outside counsel, and then speaks in precisely measured terms.

". . . please inform the other side that we are not persuaded that the Requirements Specification is precise on the issue. The Requirements Specification at page 15, Art. 6. 3. a) iii is in fact sufficiently imprecise so as to allow for a degree of interpretation, a point clearly made at page 21, Art. 3.2 a) ii of the Performance Specification provided by our clients to the plaintiff and dated . . . even if the Requirements Specification had been precise on the specific issue, which we deny, the Performance Specification makes clear that in order for our clients to provide the deliverables in accordance with the Requirements Specification . . . certain dependencies stipulated by our clients . . . were required to be performed in advance by the plaintiff before the Requirement Specification could be fulfilled by our clients . . . consequently . . . "

He does not falter, has no need to repeat himself. Then he nods to Miss Flynn, makes a note on the file, throws it to the floor, and so on and so forth.

He grinds through the day in this manner; he's known at the Hartford as the grindingest guy on executive row. He works relentlessly. Eyes and hands. Words and paper. A man composed of eyes and hands, words and paper.

Occasionally he pushes the files away, glances at the table by the door on which stand his prints, his books or his exotic teas, all the refined *bric a brac* recently ordered from various locations around the world which he will never visit in person. Then he reaches into the bottom left hand drawer of his desk and again scribbles words on to a piece of paper. He re-reads the words set out there, stares at the figures on the scrap of paper, throws the scrap into the drawer.

A little later Harry Williams, chief executive of the Hertford, puts his head through the office doorway.

"Have you read the *Courant* yet? That war matter we've had some involvement in – the *Manhattan Project* - it's come through . . ."

He holds up his arm, large palm outwards, does not look up from the file.

"Sorry Harry, not now, I'm right in the middle of this . . ."

Harry, who should know by now the abrupt business manner of his old colleague, stops in mid-sentence, looks at the impenetrable wall of neatly combed white hair and steel-grey suit, frowns, speaks up again.

"Goddammit, must you treat me like one of your clerks . . . ?"

A pause.

The white hair tilts; he looks up from his work, clearly irritated, though the voice is modulated.

"Harry, you know I have no practical interest in the Government side of the business; if I need to sign papers, send them through to Miss Flynn. Now I must get through this today . . ."

He stares at Harry Williams for a few moments, impenetrable, says nothing more, looks down at the papers in front of him.

Harry Williams looks again at the neatly combed white hair, mutters something under his breath, turns sharply on his heel.

The lawyer is so deep in his work that he does not think of his noonday walk until 1.30 pm, before immediately forgetting it again. It is only later, mid afternoon, when he looks up.

It is three o'clock.

He moves over to the table by the door, selects a packet of tea, moves with the same measured stride out of the office, moves smoothly along executive row, goes downstairs to the basement.

He brews the tea, savouring the exotic aromas filling the bare and somehow desolate room. He moves across to the one plastic table, sits down heavily, reaches into his coat pocket for the copy of the *Hartford Courant*. His eyes flick over the article:

TRUMAN DRAMATICALLY ANNOUNCES
SUCCESSFUL USE OF ATOMIC BOMB

Aboard USS Augusta. With President Truman, Aug 6 – (AP.) . . . release of first atomic bomb over Hiroshima . . ."We have just dropped a bomb on Japan which has more power than 20,000 tons of TNT. It was an overwhelming success." . . . crew's reception of the news was uproarious. The word heard on every hand was,

"I guess I'll get home sooner now."

*

He is sitting in summer shirtsleeves in his favourite armchair in the main room of his house. It is early evening. A crude brightness, harsh glare, invades the wide windows in the sparely furnished living room. He notes lazily that the old skin is peeling from the healing wound on his right arm, thorn inflicted. Red roses are festooned everywhere, spilling over every flat surface around the space he sits in. The post-mortem scent of flowers is almost overwhelming. President Truman's voice is in the room . . .

" . . . *With this bomb we have now added a new and revolutionary increase in destruction to supplement the growing power of our armed forces . . . It is an atomic bomb. It is a harnessing of the basic power of the universe. The force from which the sun draws its power has been loosed*"

He stares at the now silent radio, the most modern device in the house. His head, his face a curious red plaster bust crowned with white hair, the thoughts deeply embedded.

71

Perhaps he thinks of Schopenhauer? Perhaps of the great river which will one day flash in the sun?

On bare scorched wood mantel an expensive black carriage clock, resplendent in its austere isolation, records the captured time.

truck

At first in the dark she can see nothing.

He has switched off the headlamps. They both step down into the freezing air.

"How far is it? I can barely see the hand in front of my face . . ."

He, taciturn, indifferent, replies,

"A few steps, straight up the slope, just keep going . . ."

The night bites cold. She has travelled far.

In this defaced town square she can see, sense, under the curious glow of the part obscured three-quarter moon, towering rubble, spattered snow, the blasted lifeless shells of buildings, some buried. She can feel the empty air. She stumbles. Before her eyes she can see one battered red shoe. Left foot. Child. She feels like she is a small girl again, just as she felt that time in the city when her mother was missing for a couple of minutes and the world became suddenly big and strange to her.

She has seen nothing but destroyed empty buildings throughout the fifteen minute drive since they entered this liberated town, the holed town sign shining white in the headlamps:

Saint-Lô

She knows the driver wants to be in his bed before the drive to Paris tomorrow.

She picks her way carefully along the edge of the icy square, dimly aware of a gap opening up in the devastated space all around her. She stops, places her doubtful feet, peers through the pale light. Rubble. Desolation. Empty air.

A faint sound comes to her ears. She thinks she can hear music. She lowers her head, as if this might allow her to hear better. Again. Yes. Violins play soft music, an arrangement she has known since her childhood. She cannot yet hear the words, though she rehearses them involuntarily in her mind.

Now she is glad she insisted. She had pressed him, practically demanded she be allowed to attend this midnight mass service.

"If we could catch a part of the Service, it would ease my mind. Tonight especially on this feast of feasts . . ."

So she had told him.

Reluctantly he has agreed to bring her here. Even now, four months in, the perfect destruction somehow half-illuminates for him a possible path forward, a more true beginning, if he can see it through.

Now opening out in front of her she can see what is left of the church; one Tower completely gone, the roof caved into the Nave; the other Tower survives forlorn against the winter night. But still people are arrayed in the pews. They stand out under the night sky in quiet defiance of the horror and brutality that has visited them here in this forsaken place.

She looks across at her travel companion, who says nothing, just as he has said almost nothing during their long drive from Dieppe through storm, frost and ice. He walks on into the ruined Nave, nods to a few people he knows, points out a place in a pew for her, steps back into shadows as the Mass proceeds.

Gentle chords from violins. Now these strangers sing the carol she has loved since she was a child, but the words of the lament are new, sung in their language which is not hers.

Douce nuit , sainte nuit
Tout est calme et lumineux . . .

Mary Crowley, matron, here to help provide hospital services to the battered people of this town, looks about her. The air is cold, freezing. There is no roof and the people gathered here speak and sing out, exposed to the open elements. Snow has piled up on the ancient stone floor. The filtered light from the big moon is supplemented by many candles set out in ranks before the altar. In truth it is the bleakest scene; the many weeks preparing herself for the reality of what she might find here have not readied her for the utter desolation of the devastated town she now witnesses for the first time.

Still they sing:

Dors dans une paix céleste
Dors dans une paix céleste

She draws her shawl closer around her shoulders, looks about for Sam, the store-man and translator, the silent man who has brought her here. She picks out his tall frame leaning back against the supported church wall. In the gloom his head appears to be downturned, staring at the floor. She has witnessed this transfixed gaze for the most part of the long hazardous drive from the coast.

He appears to be unmoved by the unearthly scene surrounding him. A curious fellow, Irish like her, Protestant from Foxrock, Trinity College man. They're known for keeping themselves to themselves, but this one is something else, completely self-absorbed.

Her keen intelligent eye is already learning to pick out the Irish volunteers from the French townsfolk. Not just the obvious few un-rationed extra pounds generally carried by her countrymen, or the country tweed overcoats, but also in the lean French townspeople there is a difference in demeanour, a sullenness, a down-staring hidden anger mixed with despair.

Men, women and children, all the men either old or nearly so, some well-dressed, some threadbare, some stand together, some stand alone, the children docile, shocked. Some weep silently. She senses that she is not welcome here, that none of the volunteers are welcome here amongst these violated people, their home a place with its soul ripped away by this War between strangers.

She is barely aware as she quietly hums the tune of the carol:

Douce nuit, sainte nuit
Fils de Dieu
La lumière pure de l'amour . . .

She looks across again at the man called Sam, the one who has driven her to this strange place, to this other world which suddenly seems to her tired mind to be almost a place outside of time itself. He stands up straight, steps out into faint light in the ruined cathedral, is staring across at the far wall of the Nave. She follows his line of sight and sees two men, more old than young, clearly local, standing against the far wall, looking around distractedly at the altar, at the waxing moon, at the depleted ranks of townspeople they have probably known all of their lives, who all sing now in a ragged harmony with these strangers from another land.

These men appear bewildered, almost beaten. She sees they are arm in arm, without affectation. Sam has seen it too and she understands that the sight of these two men causes him agitation. He brings his hands up to his face and shields his eyes the better to absorb this stray image, a look of dismay, of realisation seems to cross over his sharp features. He steps back into the shadows.

The final words of the carol approach; the last grace notes of the violins fade away into the night.

Jésus le sauveur est né

There is a slight shuffling in the pews, a cough here and there. The Mass is drawing to a close. The priest is busy at the altar, moving this object, closing that curtain. Now he steps out in front of the altar to give the final blessing:

Benedícat vos omnípotens Deus,
Pater, et Fílius, et Spíritus Sanctus

With sadness he bids them go in peace to love and serve the Lord, sends them back out into their ruined world. Without clamour, as if suspended between time and place, the makeshift congregation begins to make its way slowly out of the ruins of the once vibrant cathedral into the devastation of the desolate town.

He waits for her.

"I shall take you to the huts. They have found me a bed for the night before I return to Paris tomorrow morning."

He is courteous, though she senses that for some reason he is affronted, put upon. In silence he drives the mile or so along the ghost roads, white shadows glittering in the truck headlights, through to the hastily built Nissan huts on the edge of the town.

He steers the truck, arms working furiously, into the bay at the front of one of the huts. Athletically he jumps down from the truck, comes around to her side, swings open the door, helps her down with a good natural grace. He unlocks the door of the hut, pushes it open, hands her the key.

The dark sky has cleared seemingly in moments. Looking up, she can now see the blue-black night laced with white-grey swirls, finest filigree, silver pulses more numerous, more vivid than she has seen at home, overarching this blasted corner of Normandy. For a moment she thinks of her late grandmother, of her grandmother at her needlepoint, all of those long hours of precise, fastidious work, making her mark bent over an open weave canvas. And as she conjures this image, Mary shivers. The night is cold. Her childhood was long ago.

Sam the driver is still agitated about something. He is looking at the ground. Suddenly he looks across at her, says gently:

"And now, I trust you got what you wanted from the Service?"

He nods to her quiet assent.

"I shall leave early in the morning, so keep well."

He says no more, springs back into the cab.

With a crunching clank of gears the truck reverses, brakes in a sudden halo of red light thrown up against the side-wall of the hut; hands and arms working furiously at the huge steering wheel, he peers through the frosted windscreen, lunges forward out onto the glistening road.

At this zero hour the truck whines, coughs, staggers...whiiiines as it pulls hard up the steep slope into the bleak beautiful ice-bound night.

red

NEW YORK SATURDAY 5 OCTOBER 1957
SOVIET FIRES EARTH SATELLITE INTO SPACE;
IT IS CIRCLING THE GLOBE AT 1800 M.P.H.;
SPHERE TRACKED IN 4 CROSSINGS OVER U.S

*

It is the part of the day he loves most; the bells of Notre Dame over in the town have just rung the angelus, have caused him to lay down his palette for a moment. He walks across the studio to the big many-paned windows with the view across red rooftops, seeks out the curious lit white dome set upon the ancient tower of the tiny Cathedral. Far away down the valley he can just about make out a thin ribbon of the Mediterranean Sea.

It is cooler here, by the open window; a gentle breeze stirs the white curtains, bids the leaves of the orange trees to whisper lightly, causes the fronds of the old date palms down in the garden to softly rise and fall. The scent of English honeysuckle, memory laden, sensuous, as if a coded call to some adventure of the senses or of a trial of the restless spirit, fills the evening air.

He can hear two voices speaking over by the gate; he cannot make out what is said, though the thought occurs to him once more – at this time of the day, late evening, before the night falls, it is curious how human voices, half-heard in the fading light, seem somehow amplified.

He moves his large head from side to side. How many hours? Three hours with no break – for the first time he realises how much his neck aches. Forty years ago, in the old town, when he lived in the policeman's house, the one opposite Ilyinskaya church, yes the white cottage with the red shutters, the same shutters upon which she would discretely knock in the late evening and whisper urgently;

"Moishe, Moishe, it's me....Let me in!!"

...he would throw open the red shutters and she would climb in through the window to him, her arms full of blue and purple flowers. How the people in the village talked! What joy they had known in those faraway times when they were young! He, a poor man's son, she, a rich man's daughter; they had nothing certain but their love and their vague plans and the conviction they would somehow make their future together, that impossible future!

He laughs silently to himself, shakes his head in wonder. Was he now still that same man? What connected him, now, to the person he had once been, or to that woman with whom he had spent so many hours so many days, so many years?

He lowers his head, lost in some reverie of her: then he looks back at the canvas standing wet upon the easel.

And now that he has reached his three score years and ten, what has he seen, what has he known?

He has seen much, known little - the hopes of the People's Revolution in Russia, living the flawed reality of the anarchy that followed – the destruction of her father's business, the daily battle of raw unrestrained ego in the places of work, in the streets the proscription of his creative work – his desperate return to Paris, those crazy days, the total absorption of all the new methods that came so easily to him in those wild days, first recognition, Bella and Ida joining him in Paris, then the growing abomination in Germany, the death of his old tutor Pen...

Ah, old gentle Yuri Pen. An artist with limitations perhaps, but still an artist to his core. A man born into poverty in the Pale, a man who opened his Vitebsk art school for men and women, boys and girls; if they could not pay they did not have to pay, a man who taught all who came to him the sum of what he had to teach – provided he saw something in their work. Brutally murdered in the middle of the night at age eighty-two. One month after a friendly note had been sent to him by a defected artist, his former pupil? A note which he did not even get to read?

Who will one day speak up for old Yehuda Pen?

...the vivid scar upon the soul of humanity which grew in Germany. How that quagmire almost swallowed him whole. That Exhibition - *Entartete Kunst* - denigrating his work, his flight with Bella to

Marseilles. The round-ups, his arrest, the escape to Lisbon, eventually to America. And there, once more a new start. Bella's death, suddenly, from some passing infection free to ravage her fading frail form mercilessly in drug-depleted New York State. Her body gone from him. Her unique scent; in the last few months her hurt haunted eyes, her tired smile, her feisty spirit exhausted by the weight of his relentless selfish drive to create, by her struggle to unlock her own creative self, by the burden of her people's fate. He hears the residue of her voice, calls up the feel of her fine hair in his hands, the memory of the gentle touch of her lips, the memory of the perfect curves of her firm soft body, her woman's full scented flesh...all gone from him, forever gone.

A gentle stream of cool air filters into the silent room.

Everything changes, only the work remains.

He knows it is better to stop chasing these tumbling thoughts. He goes back to the easel, takes up his palette again. For a few moments, in passing, just before the wider canvas disappears and he is focussed again upon the few square millimetres of space that requires his absolute and urgent concentration, he absorbs the work so far. Clowns, musicians, men and women, caught up in a swirl of grey and blueblack thick impasto, their faces desolate, their flutes and bugles held before them as if they walk through a fog, a dash of yellow, a swirl of red, a green hue upon a face, what colour there is constrained, as if ashamed, repressed, as if these figures are lost souls, rootless, in despair, as if they have witnessed some event they had not wanted to see; but still they play on, they play their music, even in light of what they have seen, even in light of what has been made known to them.

At centre left a singer; she is raised up by a strange birdlike creature which turns towards the centre of the work. Roughly crowned with a splosh of red hair, the creature extends yellow fingers as it listens to the lament of the violin...it is the figure of the violin-player at centre right which must have his sole attention. A ghostwhite face beneath a Fedora hat. One ghost hand places the bow over the body of the violin, itself the same grey white as the youthful face. Each eye of the ghost face is a black hole sunk deep into the socket. Now the artist looks again at the rim of the right eye; slowly, carefully, he traces a ragged white line jagging around the rim, accentuating the depth of the blackness. He repeats the procedure with the left eye; now the jagged white line is a triangle with one extended axis. He picks up another brush; beneath the ragged rim of the blackness of the right eye he extends the circumference of the rim so that a circle is created, to convey the blackness of the eye and the black shadow that sits under it. He stares hard at the square centimetre he has just completed.

The artist turns away, deep in thought, morose. There is tragedy in his work. He will one day say of it:

'Painting is a tragic language.'

There is an insistent tapping at the window. He lifts his head suddenly, goes back to it. A broad grey-green palm frond brushes against the frame. He throws the casement windows wide open and a soft gentle all-enveloping gush of warm air, scent-infused, flows into the room; near and far many birds are singing. He looks out into the shadowed garden. Sensuous. Sensual. Moment by moment.

Slowly the cooler air reasserts itself.

The luxurious scent has faded. All of those years ago, when they had first met - his wild leap towards Paris, his return full of hope for his work, a hope destroyed by war; their union; the first series recording it - the exquisite gentleness of what they had known, the quiet peace and freedom of wild passion in and of themselves alone, together, seeking each other, the painting with the brooch, her pink hat, their closed eyes, their bodies enveloped, what they had known in their secret world when they found each other...and now the memory of her, these evenings. He works alone; she watches over him, a silhouette only. The work he created when he first came to this villa; the almost suffocating red, the two of them, he and Bella, floating in red, deep red, before blue and the innocence of a proffered bouquet.

Looking up, high up into the clear firmament, he sees a tiny silver object pass high over the villa, from right to left, moving at great velocity.

In light of what he now knows, in light of what we all now know, he feels that something is gone from the face of the earth.

Tomorrow he will begin again.

midnight riff

Click

[Abstract multi-coloured shapes move across a laptop screen in various random directions. Apart from the white cursor arrow, there are two blue buttons, one at bottom left corner of the screen and one at bottom right corner of the screen. The button to left is marked 'Contribute'. The button to right is marked 'Mute'.

At first nothing can be heard.
Then mufflled sounds; voices in a distant room. A cough; one voice speaks:]

Convener: *[on-mic]* Hallo to you all, my name is Martha and I am your Convener for this call. [*beep beep beep beep*] Over in the New York office it is five to midnight and here in London it is five to five in the morning. [*beep beep*] I can hear we still have many callers dialling in! [*beep beep beep beep*] Welcome back to *World Philosophy Inc.* In this call we cover Part Three of the series, 'What consitutes a happy life, a good life?' [*beep beep beep beep*] A little housekeeping first. [*beep beep beep beep*] As we get underway and once I throw the conference into *Contribute* mode, if you wish to speak, please click on the *Contribute* button on the screen in front of you. This will allow you to speak to the entire audience [*beep beep beep*] and will also indicate your name [*beep*] or user name [*beep beep*] to those members of the audience listening through their laptop or via mobile phone. Whilst the Chairperson [*beep*] is speaking a **Chairperson: [on mic]** icon will flash up as I am now demonstrating; when the Chairperson is on mute, a **Chairperson: [off mic]** icon will appear like this one on your screen now. When I speak, or stop speaking, a **Convener: [on-mic] [off-mic]** icon as appropriate will show on your screen, as hopefully is the case now. Your Chairperson tonight [*beep*] is Ms Eva Primavera [*beep beep beep beep*]. Ms Primavera needs no introduction from me [*beep*] suffice it to say her best-selling book **Power Play: (From Zero to Nero in Five Simple Steps)** [*beep beep*] has sold out on four continents and has been translated into twenty languages [*beep beep beep*] So, on that note I wish

82

you an interesting call [*beep*] and I now hand this across to Ms Primavera.
. . [*beep beep*]

Chairperson: [on-mic] Thank you so much Martha! Hi Everybody. My,
but we have a cast of thousands this evening! Sorry for the ungodly
hour for so many listeners! Let me first explain something to you all; for
technical [*beep beep beep*] reasons we are unable this evening to welcome
our intended contributors [*beep beep*] beyond the U.S.A and Europe. We
apologise for this [*beep beep beep beep*]; it's such a shame our full global
audience cannot be with us tonight, because we had timed the call so that
we have as diverse an audience as possible, allowing all to take part and
make their own unique and invaluable contributions. But we'll record
this and will revisit the question down the line; all will have their say with
World Philosophy Inc.!

OK, so let's get straight into it.

Many of you will have read Cicero's *On the Good Life* in which
he talks to a friend about life in general, and poses the question: 'What
makes us happy, how do we live a good life?' Well, that is the continuing
subject of this series of calls.

So let's start by summarising what appears to be the position of
the great man himself. Perhaps he suggests that we are entitled to describe
the condition of the soul as peaceful when no agitation disturbs its tranquility; that there is no denying that people who have no fears or distresses
or desires or immoderate pleasures are happy?

Jan from Amsterdam: That is merely a proposition to be challenged, and
Cicero himself challenges it!

Lucia from Rome: Challenges it by means of circumlocution, digression
and prevarication only, it seems to me.

New York Don: Surely you are not suggesting that the great man himself
was capable of such...?

Simone de Paris: He said this tranquility is, for example, dependent upon
the future of his health, the durability of his luck...

Chairperson: [on-mic] Order please, Ladies and Gentlemen! Might I suggest we start this in another place - with a story? Just the other day a good
friend of mine asked me the very question: "Eva, what makes us happy
in life?" We were sitting in my garden at the time, breathing good clean
air, listening to birdsong, enjoying all the many colours surrounding us. It
seemed to me her question might be best answered by way of analogy. So I
said to my friend, 'I was sitting in this garden just last week. As you know,

Rob and I, we've made this garden a haven, a place of security for our children, here they can play safe, keep strong and thrive.'

John in London: errr. . . that's a great aim in life. . .

Chairperson: [on-mic] Thank you so much John. . . Martha, can I suggest that I'm allowed to set out the main ideas behind my thinking before others come in with their contributions?

John in London: Sorry Ms Primavera, a little trigger-happy there, I clicked on the *contribute* button by mistake!

Chairperson: [on-mic] No problem!. . . So my friend acknowledged the beauty of my garden. I said to her, 'As I was sitting here just last week, a man's face appeared looking over the fence down at the bottom of the garden'.

Brummie Blue: What's he up to then?

Chairperson: [on-mic] Hey Martha, can you block out all interruptions at this early stage of the call, so I can get the main ideas across at the start, then we can circle back around to the key proposition?

Convener: [on-mic] I thought I'd done that already! OK, listen in everybody, for now there will be no more contributions until I formally throw the call live again. OK? Thank you.

Chairperson: [on-mic] Thank you!. . . To continue, this man, he's standing at our fence just staring into our garden for at least ten minutes . . . so now I'm watching him, what will he do next? Rob is away, the small orchard we've created is teeming with fruit, I'm unsettled. . . this man, he starts to climb over the fence into my garden . . .

Convener: [off-mic] Hey, now he's out of order, this is your home!

Chairperson: [on-mic] I'm sorry? Who said that?

Convener: [on-mic] Me, Martha. I'm so sorry, I thought I was on mute!

Chairperson: [off-mic] Could you please just concentrate on your job and allow me to make my point?

Convener: [off-mic] I did say I was sorry. . .

Chairperson: [off-mic] Just do your job, it's simple enough, and allow me to do mine *[on-mic]* So the man climbs over the fence into my garden. Now I've got to consider my options. . .

Texas Pete: Me, I'd reach for my baseball bat.

Lucy in Cambridge: A typical male reaction!

Texas Pete: My apologies for living.

Chairperson: [on-mic] Martha, I thought I asked you to block other contributors for now?

Convener: [on mic] I thought I had done just that. I'm so sorry, I must

have clicked on the wrong button on my virtual console or something
Chairperson: *[off-mic]* for Christ's sake *[on-mic]* So, do I go talk to this man? Do I call for the police?. . . I hesitate. There are laws about these things . . . so I reach for my phone.
Brummie Blue: Get the law in. That's always an option
Chairperson: *[on-mic]* Sorry? Martha, if you would be so kind?. . . as I begin to dial, I see the man, unperturbed, wander up to an apple tree. The man takes a few apples from the fruit-teeming tree . . .
Minnesota Jack: So now he's a thief!
Chairperson: *[off-mic]* Can somebody get hold of Martha and tell her to do her goddamn job? *[on-mic]* So the man, he puts the apples into a canvas bag he carries. He strokes the tree in a curious movement.
Texas Pete: Wow. That's just wierd.
Chairperson: *[on-mic]* The man quietly goes back to the fence, climbs over and leaves the garden . . . OK, at this point we can throw the call open. *If you could be so kind Martha?. . .* So what lessons might my friend have drawn from my little analogy?
Karim in Harlow: Is that it? The end of the story?
Chairperson: *[on-mic]* Yes, that's the end of the story
New York Don: I cannot hear much of Cicero in any of that...
Karim in Harlow: What's the point of the story then?
Chairperson: *[on-mic]* It's an illustration of the dilemma.
Karim in Harlow: What dilemma?
Chairperson: *[on-mic]* It's about borders at every level - collective and personal, the world and the self, protect yourself, give of yourself, open yourself out to the world, the risk of transgression, the risk of disturbing the tranquility of the soul; an illustration of the dilemma inherent in the question: what makes us happy? what constitutes a good life?
Alan in Tuxford: So what does your friend think?
Chairperson: *[on-mic]* My friend?
Alan in Tuxford: Yes, you know, the one sitting with you in your big garden, the well-stocked garden teeming with fruit trees, the garden that you and Rob have spent years cultivating for the security of your children?
Chairperson: *[on-mic]* Oh yes . . . well, she said to me, "I think you need razor wire around the top of your fence." Ha ha. Well of course, I laughed at her response.
Lucy in Cambridge: You laughed at her?
Chairperson: *[on-mic]* Not at her, but at her response.
Lucy in Cambridge: Is there a difference?

Chairperson [on-mic] Yes, of course. Merely to provoke her thinking, I asked her if it might be more appropriate if I built a gate into the fence and threw it open to all at harvest time . . .

Karim in Harlow: Why would you do that?

Chairperson: [on-mic] This man who climbed over my fence into my garden, he caused me no harm . . . I may even have contributed to his happiness by cultivating the apple tree . . . that thought in turn might make me happy.

Texas Pete: Yeah, well if you say so...that's just him, what about the next guy who stares into your garden in that way?

Brummie Blue: Take no chances, that's what my life has taught me.

Chairperson: [off-mic]: Who the hell vetted the contributors for this call?*[on-mic]* So, even sitting in our quiet garden, the world presents me with dilemmas. Should we have a garden when others don't? Perhaps we should give up the garden if it is a source of potential unhappiness? And if we give it up, will it render void our sacrifice of vital years in the pursuit of it? My partner, Rob, he sometimes wants to wear bast shoes and a robe and go walking from home to Rome . . .

Brummie Blue: I think you might find it's impossible to walk to Rome from New York you know.

Chairperson: [off-mic]: Just block every other voice that has so far con-tributed to this call bar mine...

Texas Pete: Now just a minute, we have the right to be heard as much as you.

Chairperson: [on-mic] I'm sorry, you heard what I said just now? I'm not on mute?

Karim from Harlow: We've heard everything you've said since the start of the call.

Chairperson: [off-mic] Can somebody sort out these goddamn technical issues and give me the space to work here?

. . .

. . .

[Before the next voice there is a strange interference on the line which continues as the voice speaks; the words sound like an old radio broad-cast, but can be clearly made out]

Pascal: All mankind's misery derives from not being able to sit alone in a quiet garden.

Chairperson: [on-mic] Who said that?

Pascal: C'est moi, Blaise Pascal, *polymathe Francais*, Mathematician, Scientist, inventor, writer, maker of wagers, Christian philosopher, *mais non*, I am not the inventor of the wheelbarrow...

Chairperson: *[on-mic]* Err ...Monsieur Pacal? .

Pascal: Oui, madame. And so, my first proposal in respect of your analogy, as you term it, is this . . .

[Again, before the next voice, interference, words heard again like an old radio broadcast, but clearly made out, and this is repeated for each long gone voice as they join the call]

Kafka: You sit in a room on your own, the door is locked, you work quietly. . . one day the world will find you, will come banging on your door.

Chairperson: *[on-mic]* Did you say your name is Kafka?

Kafka: I said no such thing.

Pascal: Perhaps I might be allowed the floor for a moment?

Chairperson: *[off-mic]* Is this some sort of joke? Can't we have a proper discussion here without these jokers, these undesirables and peasants butting their heads in?

Brummie Blue: You aint got rid of us yet, lady.

Chairperson: *[off-mic]:* . . . I don't know what the hell is going on here. . . are they listening to every goddamn word I'm saying? Can somebody in this outfit tell me if I am on goddamn mute or not? I am? Definitely? Right. Block that Brummie Blue person, he's such an *asshole*! Get rid of the other jokers too or I'm out of here...

Brummie Blue: Oy, I heard that . . .

Pascal: If I might be allowed to speak . . .

Thomas Mann: The war for the soul of humanity, though necessary, is ruinous; an antimony typical of this vale of tears . . .

Chairperson: *[on-mic]* What did you say your name is? To which war do you refer?

Thomas Mann: My name is Thomas Mann. The war to which I refer is the war fought between the will to life and the creative temperament, permanently.

Chairperson: *[on-mic]* I'm sorry, I don't quite understand. Are you in some way related to the German writer of the past?

Thomas Mann: I know of no other German writer called Thomas Mann.

Chairperson: *[off-mic]:* Just what in hell is going on here? Is this some sort of elaborate hoax? Look – I'm prepared to humour these jokers for five more minutes – if it doesn't improve I'm closing the whole thing down – understood? *[on-mic:]* Herr Mann, your thought was nicely expressed . . . but err, what do you mean exactly?

Thomas Mann: It is indeed a precise formulation, perhaps even a little too neatly expressed. But I am afraid if those in this discussion do not intuitively grasp what I say, I may never be able to explain it.

Pascal: Oui, it's true; the heart has its reasons, which reason does not know...We know truth, not only by the reason, but also by the heart.

Chairperson: [on-mic] What was that...? No, no of course I understand Herr Mann, I merely hoped to provoke a discussion. And what, *professore,* do you think is the nature of the war you mentioned?

Thomas Mann: Why but it has a million forms . . .

Jan from Amsterdam: What has any of this got to do with Cicero?

Brummie Blue: The Chairperson's lost it for me . . . and I've made a formal complaint, I have.

Lucy in Cambridge: Some people on here are starting to gang up against Eva. It's not her fault some contributors are playing games and the technology's gone nuts!

John in London: I agree with Lucy, give Eva a break!

Wordsworth: We should be striding the storm-blasted ridges, not stuck in an office at midnight...

Thomas Mann: If I might return to the purpose of the call? Apropos Cicero's *The Good Life,* and before we begin our proper analysis of Ms Primavera's analogy, we might ask what the role of the artist might be in all of this?

New York Don: Cicero would not have understood the concept of artist as we understand it

Radical: Consider only the old sad story of Van Gogh. Now his work is priceless - a brute victory trophy signifying material dominion.

middleman: Mister, if it don't sell and there is no market - it don't get seen or heard. Shoot yourself in a field – market; end of story.

Van Gogh: So much winning and losing in the world.

colin compound's hardware emporium: . . . ¶¶be sure to buy your every need from our one floor store! ¶¶what could matter, more than matter, what could matter more?!¶¶

Convener: [on-mic] Please bear with us everybody, we are clearly having one or two technical problems.

Chairperson: [off-mic] . . . do I have mute now? Do I have mute? Yes, I'm on mute? Was that a goddamn jingle I just heard? *A freakin' jingle?* Right. Martha, are you doing this on purpose? Maybe you should be looking for something else that better suits your abilities?

Karim from Harlow: Hey, no need for that, there are technical gremlins in the works, anybody can hear that.

Mary@AllSouls: That's so unfair. Why are you giving Martha such a hard time? She's just trying to do her job.

Paolo: It often seems to me that those who wield power in the world are the people least qualified to exercise it.

Francesca: Oh Paolo, Paolo, Paolo....

Mary@AllSouls: I have no interest in power, nor any wish to impose my thoughts or my ways upon anybody, I just want to do the best I can in the time I have.

Elite Rep: Ha! Ha! Perfect, get on with it then.

Pascal: I refuse to take any further active part in this farrago. I shall now go on mute, *permanently* . . .

Chairperson: [on mic] ...   .Has anybody heard my voice for the last minute or so? We have technical problems at this end. I would like to bring a little order back to the proceedings.

Juggler: Bring on the artists and writers, we need to go into the dark.

Chairperson: [on-mic] Can anybody hear my voice? This is madness. If I can bring the call back to the real world?

Juggler: The real world? What has this discussion got to do with the real world?

... ...
... ...
... ...

a.l.kennedy: Every hedge fund manager out there continues to harness their interior moral vacuums to hoover in the wealth, the light and the sanity of the world.

Francis Stonor Saunders: Everyone has a verified self, an identity, formed through and confirmed by identification that is attested to be 'true'. Your identity is being trafficked and traded, with your permission, by interested parties about whom you know nothing.

Pope: The globalisation of indifference makes us all 'unnamed'; responsible, yet nameless and faceless.

Francis Stonor Saunders: The refugee boat overturned. An unknown pregnant woman drowned; whilst drowning she gave birth. The baby drowned also. The name of the woman who drowned was Yohanna.

. . .
. . .
. . .

. . .

Convener: There seems to be a sudden silence on the call. There are some technical problems. Are we all still connected?

. . .

. . .

. . .

. . .

Heidegger: The power of human thought to bring the far image into our immediate near vision.

Artist: And our capacity to imagine terror.

Texas Pete: It's well past midnight here.

Lucy in Cambridge: We are still in the dark on this side of the ocean.

arial: What the wild wind whispered...

. . .

. . .

. . .

. . .

. . .

Chairperson: [on-mic] For some reason I understand those on the call could not hear my voice for the last few moments. And I could not hear those on the call. We're experiencing some technical problems at this end. Can I please bring some order back to the call?

saxplayer: What the hell? It's the economy, stupid! What's the economic argument? This stuff, it just don't butter no parsnips!

teen@17: He's missing the point. Tell him it ain't so Joe . . .

Schopenhauer: "...butter no parsnips?" Ah! Money, capital, the brute lubricant! Happiness in abstracto. Consider the world as will and idea.

colin compound's hardware emporium: . . . ¶¶be sure to buy your every need from our one floor store! ¶¶what could matter, more than matter, what could matter more?!!¶¶

Texas Pete: does anybody else on here keep hearing that crazy shop jingle?

Lucy from Cambridge: I do. It's quite catchy...

Chairperson: [on-mic] Can *anybody* hear me out there? [***off-mic***] Did I hear that friggin sales jingle again just now? It's all running amok. Cut this call right now! I'm out of here. Get your goddamn boss into this office right now, *right now!*

Mary@AllSouls: Oh dear. I fear tempers are getting a little frayed in the New York office. I do wish Eva had been given the chance to develop her analogy without being distracted by all these interventions from men.

Chairperson: *[off-mic]* It's of no interest to me if you're the CEO, CFO, CTO, COO or the goddamn man in the frigging moon, you'll be hearing from my lawyers, you absolute and complete utter moron, you *asshole*!

Texas Pete: Jeez, sounds like it's all gone nuclear up there.. Was that a door slammin just now? Or maybe somebody's head bangin on a desk . . ?

Schopenhauer: Ah yes. The nuclear question. The animal drive to life is all. To seek power and to wield it. We are essentially brutes with a little creative capacity.

teen@17: Tell me it ain't so, Joe!

Schopenhauer: Arthur, not Joe. But ja, I fear this is our human predicament.

The Voice of Eloquent Discourse: That claim is a disgraceful outrage... I am not a brute!!

Sceptic: We are free to live the life we choose.

Juggler: You speak the truth. I choose the reconstructive powers of creative imagination in the face of reality.

Man of Avon:	*When I have seen such interchange of state,*
	Or state itself confounded to decay;
	Ruin hath taught me thus to ruminate
	That Time will come and take my love away

Brummie Blue: A Midlands voice! South east of Birmingham by the sound of it. Lovely words too...deep words my Alice would have said, if she were still with us.

the Voice of Eloquent Discourse: This is all histrionic inelegant undignified nonsense.

Mary@AllSouls: Inelegant? Undignified? Is this an elegant dignified world?

JJ: *Tranquillo!* This has become a funferall, a riff on a theme, it will all be forgotten tomorrow.

Mary@AllSouls: Well, just like those refugees I guess . . . they are forgotten the moment we flip to the next channel. The woman Yohanna stays in my mind. Who cares for her?

Juggler: I care. I do care. Yet the one thing I can do, like others, is name her. Yohanna.

Mary@AllSouls: Well, I just wanted to say, it all gets lost in the noise sometimes, we should think on . . .

JJ: To imagine her terror...No. Life is not a fun for all, nor indeed for any of us, not when the cold wind blows.

Beckett: And when did the cold wind stop blowing?

JJ: How are you Mr Beckett? Did you complete your work eventually?

Beckett: In my own way. You say it is a riff. I say it is a fugue. A main subject taken up by others and interweaving. Also hysterics; we have lost our way.

colin compound's hardware emporium: . . . ¶¶be sure to buy your every need from our one floor store! ¶¶what could matter, more than matter, what could matter more?!!!¶¶

The Voice of Good Sense: Open the windows!! Let's get some fresh air in here!!!

Chairperson [on-mic]: OK everybody. Listen up now.

Texas Pete: Eva's back!

Lucy In Cambridge: Great you've made it back on the call, Eva!

Chairperson: [on-mic]: Enough. One last word from me, before I get the hell out of here. I've heard what you've all had to say. Especially the old voices, with your twisty thoughts and your lofty lamentations, whoever or whatever the hell you are. Let me tell you something straight. Your time has gone. Over. Finished. Dis-ap-pearo. You've made your contribution, now step aside and get off the bus. Pale. Male. Ego. Vanity of vanities. And you want to know something else? Whilst you were suffering your great excruciations, giving the world the benefit of your vast thoughts torn deep from your despairing soul, the world just kept straight on down the road to hell. Nobody listened. Nobody cared. Not one thing changed as a result of your work. You people just filtered off the excess human spirit of an age, you were never anything more than the exhaust pipe of the frenetic juggernaut which is the engine of capitalism. Meanwhile those who really run the show just kept on robbing the Bank, one way or the other. Now your work provides tenure for a thousand professors, who treat it like some secret language discovered on ancient tablets buried in the desert, an artefact of no relevance to our daily lived lives. And having poured over your works, the theorists, those Frenchmen and their disciples, they finally figured it out - it was them, the theorists, and us, the readers – we all wrote your books! And now the world accepts this theory as truth. Your time is over; period. Gone: *finito*. There's a new bus coming down the road, going to a new place – new voices will have their say; voices which will bring gifts prejudices fears victimhoods certainties flaws doubts hopes dreams aspirations, fluid selves. New voices. A new time. A new way. The safe privilege, the learned narratives of one moment in history – it's gone. It's your choice guys; get back on the bus and sit quietly at the back or stand clear of the doors. It is this thought which makes me happy – the thought of these new voices forging a new path to the waterfall.

O.K. that's me done, I'm out of here....

[beeeeeeeeep]

Pascal: *Mon Dieu!* The final debacle!
Thomas Mann: I say only this; our considered fictions provided a rare access to truth, an access not manipulated by those in power in the world. Where else in these times do you find such access to truth? As for those French theorists and their disciples - if a meteorologist is allowed to tamper with the mainspring of the finest timepiece, you must expect some fluctuation in its performance.
JJ: Lighten up, Tommy boy! Spoken like the true son of a burgher of Lübeck! In life, live and let live. We are all, men and women of every caste and hue, poleing our punt up the Orinoko and that distant roar is the Angel Falls beyant! In truth 'tis the deepest place. Well then, but didn't I tell you?
Juggler: Or maybe it's just like Goose Fair on Forest Fields. A funfair. A palaver from start to finish...
French Theorist: You wear disguises, speak in riddles, as if you pursue some hidden aim.
Juggler: *Bravo Monsieur!* You rang the bell and you win the prize! Feel free to pick up your stuffed donkey on the way out of the tent - and be sure to take it with you! But before you go answer me this, my Sorbonne scholar; if a madman took a sledgehammer to Michelangelo's *Pieta* and smashed it to smithereens, could you and the rest of the world remake it?
French Theorist: We spoke of literature, not sculpture.
Juggler: You spoke of art, of artists, of what they might know and might not know.
Camus: Listen my friend. I wrote my books; so much is clear. But my work without a gifted reader is nothing. Such readers seek truth. A true work of art extends the horizon of our inner freedom.
Juggler: You left us too soon.
Mary@AllSouls: And still they blather on. Good for Eva. She told it straight as she sees it. Maybe she's right too, who knows? Though I don't see that juggernaut slowing down any time soon, whoever holds the mic. Unless it goes over the cliff once and for all. What then? Let's hope some new tyranny isn't forming around us as we speak. Now it's been a long call,

my thoughts grow lazy...are we near the end?

... ...

... ...

Convener: *[on-mic]* Hi all, this is Martha. I'm sorry, my kids called me away. I thought I should step back in now. I apologise for the technical problems we've been experiencing today, it's all been way beyond my control. . . I hear my children calling again, they're awake, I need to go to them...

[Beep beep beep beep]

... ...

... ...

Oliver "Babe" Hardy: Well, here's another nice mess you've gotten me into...

... ...

... ...

Convener: *[on-mic]* O.K I'm back. For some reason the Chairperson appears to have left us all alone so I'll wrap it up. Thank you all. Join *World Philosophy Inc.* same time next month for Part Four of the series.

[beep beep beep beep beep beep beep]

Convener: *[on-mic]* What's that big red ball in the sky?

... ...

Mary@AllSouls: Are you still there, Martha? Was that your kid's voice we heard just now?

Convener: *[on-mic]* Sssh, sssh, go back into your room, I'll come to you soon . . .Sorry to anybody still on the call, that was my three year old daughter Hannah paying us a visit . . . hey...can I share something with you all for a moment? I've decided to break free from these people and do my own thing from here on...and I'll start right now by trying to describe to you all what I can see just at this moment...Dawn is breaking on this side of the ocean . . . from my window high up on the seventeenth floor here in east London, I look out over a wide curve of the river Thames . . . there is fog in patches over the river, just lifting...I can see the first rays of the sun as it clears the horizon . . . high above the streets, above the traffic's noise, beyond the cable cars and the high-rise apartment blocks just now enflamed by the early light of the sun - their red warning lamps still glowing - beyond the day's first ferries carrying so many souls on their next journey to a new place, beyond the wake of the solitary pilot's boat .

. . I can see the new light pick out a few green fields...I lift my eyes to the low hills above Greenwich and far beyond I imagine the river reach out to the sea . . . you know, I just wanted to say, it is a simple thing, a wonderful terrible thing, to witness the arrival of the early morning sun.

This is your Convener, signing off for the last time.

cheers *[beep beep]* thank you *[beep beep]* you take good care now *[beep beep]* look after those kids *[beep beep beep]* ciao *[beep beep beep]* au revoir *[beep beep]* adios *[beep]* sayonara *[beep beep]* auf wiedersehen *[beep beep]* farvel *[beep beep]* proschay *[beep]* until the next time *[beep]* goodbye *[beep beep]* goodbye goodbye *[beep beep beep]* adieu *[beep]* adieu...adieu...adieu *[beeeeeeeeeeeeeepp]*

This call has now finished.

Click.

wonder - Aneiran is the poet of *Y Goddodin*, a traditional Old Welsh hero/ warrior poem which recounts the battle of Catreath, where three hundred British warriors were massacred by the Saxons in Northumbria in c. 596/597, and of which Aneiran was the reputed sole survivor. Augustine was sent by Rome to convert the English (i.e Anglo Saxons) to Christianity in 597.

Torquino's Question - The poet Dante visited San Gimignano, Italy for the purpose stated in the story in 1300. A memorial stone in the Sala di Dante in San Gimignano gives the actual year of the visit as 1299, although all other references I have seen suggest 1300 as the correct date.

gateway – Chaucer, in historical fact, lived above Aldwych Gate in London, the main entry point into London for the Peasants Revolt in 1381. This story imagines, amongst other things, how Chaucer may have had the first ideas for the *Wife of Bath's Prologue & Tale*.

voyager – 'True Reportory. . . ' a letter concerning the shipwreck of the *Sea Venture* off Bermuda in 1609 by William Strachey is understood by most to be a source for Shakespeare's *The Tempest*. Strachey lived, for a period, in the nascent English Colony in Virginia.

hero - When walking in the Ullswater Valley, I was told the poet Wordsworth was sitting in the White Lion at Patterdale when he heard of the victory at the Battle of Trafalgar.

wave - Popov is credited (by some sources, not all) with the first transmission of a message by radio waves in 1896. The Russian writer Chekhov was, amongst other things, completing his play *The Seagull* in the same week.

jj reads the evening paper - On the day Archduke Franz Ferdinand was assassinated, the Irish writer James Joyce was in Trieste, then on the eastern border of the Austro-Hungarian Empire.

fall - After the Reichstag was burnt down in 1933, the writer Thomas Mann was exiled from Germany. On the date described in the story, the writer was in Arosa, but the events described in the story are fictional.

king of the sun - Wallace Stevens, the American poet, was also a corporate lawyer. Here events in his life are imagined on the day the first atom bomb was dropped. The sun is a strongly recurrent image in Stevens's work.

truck – In late 1945 Samuel Beckett worked as a hospital administrator and truck driver in the French town of Saint-Lo, destroyed by allied air strikes following the D Day landings. At Christmas Eve 1945 he attended a midnight mass with Mary Crowley, an Irish Red Cross worker he had collected from the coast that day.

red – the painter Marc Chagall was caught up in the Russian Revolution and the Second World War amongst many other events in his long life. On 4th October 1957, the Soviet Union launched the Sputnik 1 satellite which completed the first orbit of earth, and continued to orbit the earth for several weeks.

midnight riff – a freewheeling bogus international conference call, to which various thinkers, politicians, artists and others contribute in a haphazard and crackpot fashion.

Acknowledgements

wonder: *for this piece I read the poem* **Y Gododdin** *in a version translated and prepared by Steve Short, LLanerch Publishers, Felinfach. The Old English poem quoted is* **The Wanderer**. *Gregory's puns and Augustine's short speech comes from Bede's* **Ecclesiastical History of the English People**. *The hawk paragraph calls up Yeats's* **The Second Coming** *(1919), though the sequence is reversed.*

 gateway: *Peter Ackroyd's* **Chaucer** *from Vintage Books provided useful background detail. The conversation with the women was suggested by* **The Wife of Bath's Prelude and Tale**.

wave; *An article by Joe McKenna on The Institute of Electrical Engineer's (USA) website and from an unclassified document from the NSA website, generally available to the public provided useful background on Popov and his radio experiments. Details of Chekhov's life on that day are suggested by David Rayfield's biography of Chekhov and from the writer's letters.*

jj reads the evening paper: *an earlier version of this vignette was published by MIROnline in May 2017*

fall: *Thomas Mann's short speech in the story is largely constructed from letters he sent at this time. See '***Letters of Thomas Mann 1889 – 1955***', selected and translated by Richard and Clara Winston; the words quoted by the fascist are from Mann's essay '***Sufferings and Greatness of Richard Wagner***', 1933, in Thomas Mann,* **Essays of Three Decades***, translated by H T*

Lowe-Porter, 1948. When writing this story I read again **Thomas Mann, Life as a Work of Art***, a biography of Mann by Hermann Kurzke*

king of the sun: *For details of Wallace Stevens's life at this time, I read* **Letters of Wallace Stevens** *published by University of California Press, and* **Parts of a World** *by Peter Brazeau; for details of the USAF flight to Hiroshima and the release and detonation of the bomb itself, I read various sources publicly available on the web which referred out to (i)* 'Ruin From The Air' *by Gordon Thomas and Max Morgan-Witts (1977) (ii) Malik, John (September 1985)* The Yields of the Hiroshima and Nagasaki Explosions *and (iii) Kerr, George D.; Young, Robert W.; Cullings, Harry M.; Christy, Robert F. (2005). "Bomb Parameters". In Young, Robert W.; Kerr, George D. Reassessment of the Atomic Bomb Radiation Dosimetry for Hiroshima and Nagasaki – Dosimetry System 2002.*

red:. *The paintings alluded to in this piece are;* '**Clowns at Night**' *(1957)* 'Lovers in Green' *(1914-15) and* 'Lovers on a Red Background' *(1950). I read Chagall's memoir* **My Life** *(1931) and Jackie Wullschlager's biography of the painter* 'Chagall Love and Exile' *in preparation for this vignette and other material generally available on the web, including from the Tate Organisation concerning the 2013 Exhibition of Chagall at the Tate, Liverpool, which I visited. The opening headline is taken from the New York Times of 5 October 1957.*

midnight riff: *quote tagged* **a.l kennedy** *is taken from an article* **"I'm Ready To Dump Broken Britain"** *by the writer and commentator a.l kennedy in the Guardian dated 31 July 2016; references attributed to* **Frances Stonor Saunders** *and the quote assigned to the* **Pope** *are from an essay by Frances Stonor Saunders called,* "**Where on earth are you**" *in the London Review of Books (LRB) dated 3 March 2016; the quote from Man of Avon is the conclusion of* **Shakespeare's Sonnet 64***; the principle behind the words tagged* **Camus** *can be found in the interview* "The Wager of Our Generation" *by Albert Camus (October 1957) from the essay collection* **Resistance, Rebellion, and Death***; generally, views expressed by contributors can be supported with reference to various works or comments by those named, given due allowance for the limitations of my own understanding.*

Finally I would like to say thank you to Dame Hilary Mantel for her pithy and kind comments on an early version of a couple of these vignettes, to Helen Vendler for her positive response and contribution to **king of the sun***, to the poet Kieron Winn and the author Will Buckingham for their respective* *responses to different drafts of **midnight riff**, my friend Mike Fegan for his knowledge of marine cannon used in **"hero"**, Suman Chakraborty at **Roman Books** for his continued support and a big thanks as always to my wife Lesley for everything she is in my life.*

about the author

Tom O'Rourke manages his time between Nottingham and London. He has degrees in literature and law. He worked for many years as an in-house commercial lawyer. His love of reading and writing preceded, endured and has survived both his brief exposure to formal literary study and his prolonged legal career.

www.ingramcontent.com/pod-product-compliance
Lightning Source LLC
Chambersburg PA
CBHW061526020726
47502CB00006B/2247